**Selected praise for
New York Times and *USA TODAY* bestselling author
Brenda Jackson**

"Brenda Jackson writes romance that sizzles
and characters you fall in love with."
—*New York Times* and *USA TODAY*
bestselling author Lori Foster

"Jackson's trademark ability to
weave multiple characters and side stories together
makes shocking truths all the more exciting."
—*Publishers Weekly*

"Possibly [the] sexiest entry
in the Westmoreland series... Jackson has
the sexiest cowboy to ever ride the range."
—*RT Book Reviews* on *A Wife for a Westmoreland*

"Jackson's characters are wonderful, strong,
colorful and hot enough to burn the pages."
—*RT Book Reviews* on *Westmoreland's Way*

"The kind of sizzling, heart-tugging story
Brenda Jackson is famous for."
—*RT Book Reviews* on *Spencer's Forbidden Passion*

"This is entertainment at its best."
—*RT Book Reviews* on *Star of His Heart*

D0171566

Dear Reader,

Wow! It's time to savor another Westmoreland. I actually felt the heat between Micah and Kalina while writing their story.

Feeling the Heat is a story of misunderstanding and betrayal. Kalina thinks Micah is the one man who broke her heart. A man she could never love again. Micah believes if Kalina really knew him she would know he could never cause her pain. So he is determined that she get to know the real Micah Westmoreland. He also intends to prove that when a Westmoreland wants something—or someone—he will stop at nothing to get it, and Micah Westmoreland wants Kalina Daniels back in his life.

Relax and enjoy Micah and Kalina's story. And with every Brenda Jackson book it is suggested that you have a cold drink ready. Be prepared to feel the heat!

Happy reading!

Brenda Jackson

BRENDA JACKSON

FEELING THE HEAT

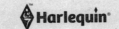

Recycling programs
for this product may
not exist in your area.

ISBN-13: 978-0-373-73162-6

FEELING THE HEAT

www.Harlequin.com

Printed in U.S.A.

Books by Brenda Jackson

Harlequin Desire

*A Wife for a Westmoreland #2077
*The Proposal #2089
*Feeling the Heat #2149

Silhouette Desire

*Delaney's Desert Sheikh #1473
*A Little Dare #1533
*Thorn's Challenge #1552
*Stone Cold Surrender #1601
*Riding the Storm #1625
*Jared's Counterfeit Fiancée #1654
*The Chase Is On #1690
*The Durango Affair #1727
*Ian's Ultimate Gamble #1745
*Seduction, Westmoreland Style #1778
*Spencer's Forbidden Passion #1838
*Taming Clint Westmoreland #1850
*Cole's Red-Hot Pursuit #1874
*Quade's Babies #1911
*Tall, Dark...Westmoreland! #1928
*Westmoreland's Way #1975
*Hot Westmoreland Nights #2000
*What a Westmoreland Wants #2035

Kimani Arabesque

†Whispered Promises
†Eternally Yours
†One Special Moment
†Fire and Desire
†Secret Love
†True Love
†Surrender
†Sensual Confessions
†Inseparable

Kimani Romance

**Solid Soul #1
**Night Heat #9
**Beyond Temptation #25
**Risky Pleasures #37
**Irresistible Forces #89
**Intimate Seduction #145
**Hidden Pleasures #189
**A Steele for Christmas #253
**Private Arrangements #269

*The Westmorelands
†Madaris Family Saga
**Steele Family titles

Other titles by this author
are available in ebook format.

BRENDA JACKSON

is a die "heart" romantic who married her childhood sweetheart and still proudly wears the "going steady" ring he gave her when she was fifteen. Because she believes in the power of love, Brenda's stories always have happy endings. In her real-life love story, Brenda and her husband of thirty-eight years live in Jacksonville, Florida, and have two sons.

A *New York Times* bestselling author of more than seventy-five romance titles, Brenda is a recent retiree who now divides her time between family, writing and traveling with Gerald. You may write Brenda at P.O. Box 28267, Jacksonville, Florida 32226, by email at WriterBJackson@aol.com or visit her website at www.brendajackson.net.

THE DENVER WESTMORELAND FAMILY TREE

Raphel and Gemma Westmoreland

Stern Westmoreland (Paula Bailey)

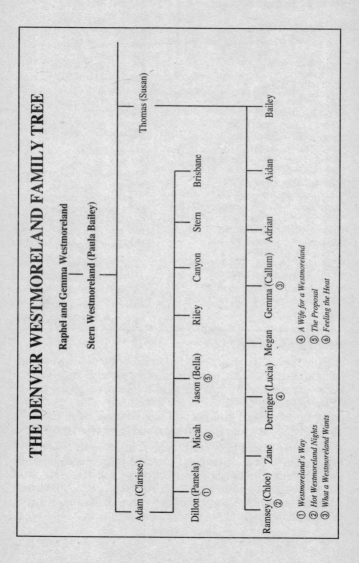

Thomas (Susan)

Adam (Clarisse)

Dillon (Pamela) ①   Micah ⑥   Jason (Bella) ⑤   Riley   Canyon   Stern   Brisbane

Ramsey (Chloe) ②   Zane   Derringer (Lucia) ④   Megan   Gemma (Callum) ③   Adrian   Aidan   Bailey

① *Westmoreland's Way*
② *Hot Westmoreland Nights*
③ *What a Westmoreland Wants*

④ *A Wife for a Westmoreland*
⑤ *The Proposal*
⑥ *Feeling the Heat*

To Gerald Jackson, Sr.
My one and only. My everything.

To all my readers who enjoy reading about the Westmorelands, this book is especially for you!

To my Heavenly Father. How Great Thou Art.

For we walk by faith, not by sight.
—*II Corinthians* 5:7

One

Micah Westmoreland glanced across the ballroom at the woman just arriving and immediately felt a tightening in his gut. Kalina Daniels was undeniably beautiful, sensuous in every sense of the word.

He desperately wanted her.

A shadow of a smile touched his lips as he took a sip of his champagne.

But if he knew Kalina, and he *did* know Kalina, she despised him and still hadn't forgiven him for what had torn them apart two years ago. It would be a freezing-cold day in hell before she let him get near her, which meant sharing her bed again was out of the question.

He inhaled deeply and could swear that even with the distance separating them he could pick up her scent, a memory he couldn't seem to let go of. Nor could he let go of the memories of the time they'd shared together while in Australia. And there had been many. Even now, it didn't take much to recall the whisper of her breath on him just seconds before her mouth—

"Haven't you learned your lesson yet, Micah?"

He frowned and shot the man standing across from him a narrowed look. Evidently his best friend, Beau Smallwood, was also aware of Kalina's entry, and Beau, more than anyone, knew their history.

Micah took a sip of his drink and sat back on his heels. "Should I have?"

Beau merely smiled. "Yes, if you haven't, then you should. Need I remind you that I was there that night when Kalina ended up telling you to go to hell and not to talk to her ever again?"

Micah flinched, remembering that night, as well. Beau was right. After Kalina had overheard what she'd assumed to be the truth, she'd told him to kiss off in several languages. She was fluent in so damn many. The words might have sounded foreign, but the meaning had been crystal clear. She didn't want to see him again. Ever. With the way she'd reacted, she could have made that point to a deaf person.

"No, you don't need to remind me of anything." He wondered what she would say when she saw him tonight. Had she actually thought he wouldn't come? After all, this ceremony was to honor all medical personnel who worked for the federal government. As epidemiologists working for the Centers for Disease Control, they both fell within that category.

Knowing how her mind worked, he suspected she probably figured he wouldn't come. That he would be reluctant to face her. She thought the worst about him and had believed what her father had told her. Initially, her believing such a thing had pissed him off—until he'd accepted that given the set of circumstances, not to mention how well her father had played them both for fools, there was no way she could not believe it.

A part of him wished he could claim that she should have known him better, but even now he couldn't make that assertion. From the beginning, he'd made it perfectly clear to her, as he'd done with all women, that he wasn't interested in a serious relationship. Since Kalina was as into her career as he'd been into his, his suggestion of a no-strings affair hadn't bothered her at all and she'd agreed to the affair knowing it wasn't long-term.

At the time, he'd had no way of knowing that she would eventually get under his skin in a way that, even now, he found hard to accept. He hadn't been prepared for the serious turn their affair had taken until it had been too late. By then her father had already deliberately lied to save his own skin.

"Well, she hasn't seen you yet, and I prefer not being around when she does. I do remember Kalina's hostility toward you even if you don't," Beau said, snagging a glass of champagne from the tray of a passing waiter. "And with that said, I'm out of here." He then quickly walked to the other side of the room.

Micah watched Beau's retreating back before turning his attention to his glass, staring down at the bubbly liquid. Moments later, he sighed in frustration and glanced up in time to see Kalina cross the room. He couldn't help noticing he wasn't the only man watching her. That didn't surprise him.

One thing he could say, no matter what function she attended, whether it was in the finest restaurant in England or in a little hole in the wall in South Africa, she carried herself with grace, dignity and style. That kind of presence wasn't a necessity for her profession. But she made it one.

It had been clear to him the first time he'd met her—that night three years ago when her father, General Neil Daniels, had introduced them at a military function here in D.C.—that he and Kalina shared an intense attraction that had foretold a heated connection. What had surprised him was that she had captivated him without even trying.

She hadn't made things easy for him. In fact, to his way of thinking, she'd deliberately made things downright difficult. He'd figured he could handle just about anything. But when he'd later run into her in Sydney, she'd almost proven him wrong.

They'd been miles away from home, working together while trying to keep a deadly virus from spreading. He hadn't been ready to settle down. While he didn't consider himself a player in the same vein as some of his brothers and cousins, women had shifted in and out of his life with frequency once they saw he had no intention of putting a ring on anyone's finger. And he enjoyed traveling and seeing the world. He had a huge spread back in Denver just waiting for the day he was ready to retire, but he didn't see that happening for many years to come. His career as an epidemiologist was important to him.

But those two months he'd been involved with Kalina he had actually thought about settling down on his one hundred acres and doing nothing but enjoying a life with her. At one point, such thoughts would have scared the hell out of him, but with Kalina, he'd accepted that they couldn't be helped. Spending time with a woman like her would make any man think about tying his life with one woman and not sowing any more wild oats.

When he'd met the Daniels family, he'd known immediately that the father was controlling and the daughter was determined not to be controlled. Kalina was a woman who liked her independence. Wanted it. And she was determined to demand it—whether her father went along with it or not.

In a way, Micah understood. After all, he had come from a big family and although he didn't have any sisters, he did have three younger female cousins. Megan and Gemma hadn't been so bad. They'd made good decisions and stayed out of trouble while growing up. But the youngest female Westmoreland, Bailey, had been out of control while following around her younger hellion brothers, the twins Aidan and Adrian, as well as Micah's baby brother, Bane. The four of them had done a number of dumb things while in their teens, earning a not-so-nice reputation in Denver. That had been years ago. Now, thank God, the twins and Bailey were in college and Bane had graduated from the naval academy and was pursuing his dream of becoming a SEAL.

His thoughts shifted back to Kalina. She was a woman who refused to be pampered, although her father was determined to pamper her anyway. Micah could understand a man wanting to look out for his daughter, wanting to protect her. But sometimes a parent could go too far.

When General Daniels had approached Micah about doing something to keep Kalina out of China, he hadn't gone along with the man. What had happened between him and Kalina had happened on its own and hadn't been motivated by any request of her father's, although she now thought otherwise. Their affair had been one of those things that just happened. They had been attracted to each other from the first. So why she would assume he'd had ulterior motives to seek an affair was beyond him.

Kalina was smart, intelligent and beautiful. She possessed the most exquisite pair of whiskey-colored eyes, which made her honey-brown skin appear radiant. And the lights in the room seemed to highlight her shoulder-length brown hair and show its luxuriance. The overall picture she presented would make any male unashamedly aware of his sexuality. As he took another sip of his drink and glanced across the room, he thought she looked just as gorgeous as she had on their last date together, when they had returned to the States. It had been here in this very city, where they'd met, when their life together had ended after she discovered what she thought was the truth. To this day, he doubted he would ever forgive her father for distorting the facts and setting him up the way he had.

Micah sighed deeply and took the last sip of his drink, emptying his glass completely. It was time to step out of the shadows and right into the line of fire. And he hoped like hell that he survived it.

Micah was here.

The smile on Kalina's face froze as a shiver of awareness coursed through her and a piercing throb hit her right between the legs. She wasn't surprised at her body's familiar reaction where he was concerned, just annoyed. The man had that sort of effect on her and even after all this time the wow factor hadn't diminished.

It was hard to believe it had been two years since she had found out the truth, that their affair in Australia had been orchestrated by her father to keep her out of Beijing. Finding out had hurt—it still did—but what Micah had done had only reinforced her belief that men couldn't be trusted. Not her father, not Micah, not any of them.

And especially not the man standing in front of her with the glib tongue, weaving tales of his adventures in the Middle East and beyond. If Major Brian Rose thought he was impressing her, he was wrong. As a military brat, no one had traveled the globe as much as she had. But he was handsome enough, and looked so darn dashing in his formal military attire, he was keeping her a little bit interested.

Of course, she knew that wherever Micah was standing he would look even more breathtaking than Major Rose. The women in attendance had probably all held their breath when he'd walked into the room. As far as she was concerned, there wasn't any man alive who could hold a candle to him, in or out of clothes. That conclusion reminded her of when they'd met, almost three years ago, at a D.C. event similar to this one.

Her father had been honored that night as a commissioned officer. She'd had her own reason to celebrate in the nation's capital. She had finally finished medical school and accepted an assignment to work as a civilian for the federal government's infectious-disease research team.

It hadn't taken her long to hear the whispers about the drop-dead-gorgeous and handsome-as-sin Dr.

Micah Westmoreland, who had graduated from Harvard Medical School before coming to work for the government as an infectious-disease specialist. But nothing could have prepared her for coming face-to-face with him.

She had been rendered speechless. Gathering the absolute last of her feminine dignity, she had picked up her jaw, which had fallen to the floor, and regained her common sense by the time her father had finished the introductions.

When Micah had acknowledged her presence, in a voice that had been too sexy to belong to a real man, she'd known she was a goner. And when he had taken her smaller hand in his in a handshake, it had been the most sensuous gesture she'd ever experienced. His touch alone had sent shivers up and down her spine and put her entire body in a tailspin. She had found it simply embarrassing to know any man could get her so aroused, and without even putting forth much effort.

"So, Dr. Daniels, where is your next assignment taking you?"

She was jerked out of her thoughts by the major's question. Was that mockery she'd heard in his voice? She was well aware of the rumor floating around that her father pretty much used his position to control her destinations and would do anything within his power to keep her out of harm's way. That meant she would never be able to go anyplace where there was some real action.

She'd been trying to get to Afghanistan for two years and her request was always denied, saying she was needed elsewhere. Although her father swore up and down he had nothing to do with it, she knew better.

Losing her mother had been hard on him, and he was determined not to lose his only child, as well. Hadn't he proven just how far he would go when he'd gotten Micah to have that affair with her just to keep her out of Beijing during the bird-flu epidemic?

"I haven't been given an assignment yet. In fact, I've decided to take some time off, an entire month, starting tomorrow."

The man's smile widened. "Really, now, isn't that a coincidence. I've decided to take some time off, too, but I have only fourteen days. Anywhere in particular that you're going? Maybe we can go there together."

The man definitely didn't believe in wasting time, Kalina thought. She was just about to tell the major, in no uncertain terms, that they wouldn't be spending any time together, not even if her life depended on it, when Brian glanced beyond her shoulder and frowned. Suddenly, her heart kicked up several beats. She didn't have to imagine why. Other men saw Micah as a threat to their playerhood since women usually drooled when he was around. She had drooled the first time *she'd* seen him.

Kalina refused to turn around, but couldn't stop her body's response when Micah stepped into her line of vision, all but capsizing it like a turbulent wave on a blast of sensual air.

"Good evening, Major Rose," he said with a hard edge to his voice, one that Kalina immediately picked up on. The two men exchanged strained greetings, and she watched how Micah eyed Major Rose with cool appraisal before turning his full attention to her. The hard lines on his face softened when he asked, "And how have you been, Kalina?"

She doubted that he really cared. She wasn't surprised he was at this function, but she *was* surprised he had deliberately sought her out, and there was no doubt in her mind he'd done so. Any other man who'd done what he had done would be avoiding her like the plague. But not Dr. Micah Westmoreland. The man had courage of steel, but in this case he had just used it foolishly. He was depending on her cultured upbringing to stop her from making a scene, and he was right about her. She had too much pride and dignity to cause a commotion tonight, although she'd gone off on him the last time they had seen each other. She still intended to let him know exactly how she felt by cutting him to the core, letting it be obvious that he was the last person she wanted to be around.

"I'm fine, and now if you gentlemen will excuse me, I'll continue to make my rounds. I just arrived, and there are a number of others I want to say hello to."

She needed to get away from Micah, and quick. He looked stunning in his tux, which was probably why so many women in the room were straining their necks to get a glimpse of him. Even her legs were shaky from being this close to him. She suddenly felt hot, and the cold champagne she'd taken a sip of wasn't relieving the slow burn gathering in her throat.

"I plan to mingle, myself," Micah said, reaching out and taking her arm. "I might as well join you since there's a matter we need to discuss."

She fought the urge to glare up at him and tell him they had nothing to discuss. She didn't want to snatch her arm away from him because they were already getting attention, probably from those who'd heard what happened between them two years ago. Unfortunately, the gossip mill was alive and well, especially when it came to Micah Westmoreland. She had heard about him long before she'd met him. It wasn't that he'd been the type of man who'd gone around hitting on women. The problem was that women just tended to place him on their wish list.

"Fine, let's talk," she said, deciding that if Micah thought he was up to such a thing with her, then she was ready.

Fighting her intense desire to smack that grin right off his face, she glanced over at Major Rose and smiled apologetically. "If you will excuse me, it seems Dr. Westmoreland and I have a few things to discuss. And I haven't decided just where I'll be going on vacation, but I'll let you know. I think it would be fun if you were to join me." She ignored the feel of Micah's hand tightening on her arm.

Major Rose nodded and gave her a rakish look. "Wonderful. I will await word on your plans, Kalina."

Before she could respond, Micah's hand tightened on her arm even more as he led her away.

"Don't count on Major Rose joining you anywhere," Micah all but growled, leaning close to Kalina's ear while leading her across the ballroom floor toward an exit. He had checked earlier and the French doors opened onto the outside garden. It was massive and far away from the ball, so no one could hear the dressing-down he was certain Kalina was about to give him.

She glared at him. "And don't count on him doing otherwise. You don't own me, Micah. Last I looked, there's nothing of yours on my body."

"Then look again, sweetheart. Everything of mine

is written all over that body of yours. I branded you. Nothing has changed."

They came to a stop in front of what was the hotel's replica of the White House's prized rose garden. He was glad no one was around. No prying eyes or over-eager ears. The last time she'd had her say he hadn't managed to get in a single word for dodging all the insults and accusations she'd been throwing at him. That wouldn't be the case this time. He had a lot to say and he intended for her to hear all of it.

"Nothing's changed? How dare you impose your presence on me after what you did," she snarled, transforming from a sophisticated lady to a roaring lioness. He liked seeing her shed all that formality and cultural adeptness and get downright nasty. He especially liked that alteration in the bedroom.

He crossed his arms over his chest. "And what exactly did I do, other than to spend two months of what I consider the best time of my life with you, Kalina?"

He watched her stiffen her spine when she said, "And I'm supposed to believe that? Are you going to stand here and lie to my face, Micah? Deny that you weren't in cahoots with my father to keep me away from Beijing, using any means necessary? I wasn't needed in Sydney."

"I don't deny that I fully agreed with your father that Beijing was the last place you needed to be, but I never agreed to keep you out of China."

He could tell she didn't want to hear the truth. She'd heard it all before but still refused to listen. Or to believe it. "And it wasn't that you weren't needed in Sydney," he added, remembering how they'd been sent there to combat the possible outbreak of a deadly virus.

"You and I worked hard to keep the bird-flu epidemic from spreading to Australia, so it wasn't just sex, sex and more sex for us, Kalina. We worked our asses off, or have you forgotten?"

He knew his statement threw her for a second, made her remember. Yes, they might have shared a bed every night for those two months, but their daytime hours weren't all fun and games. No one except certain members of the Australian government had been aware that their presence in the country had been for anything other than pleasure.

And regardless of what she'd thought, she had been needed there. He had needed her. They had worked well together and had combated a contagious disease. He had already spent a year in Beijing and had needed to leave when his time was up. Depression had started to set in with the sight of people dying right before his eyes, mostly children. It had been so frustrating to work nonstop trying unsuccessfully to find a cure before things could get worse.

Kalina had wanted to go to Beijing and get right in the thick of things. He could just imagine how she would have operated. She was not only a great epidemiologist, she was also a compassionate one, especially when there was any type of outbreak. He could see her getting attached to the people—especially the children—to the point where she would have put their well-being before her own.

That, and that alone, was the reason he had agreed with her father, but at no time had he plotted to have an affair with her to keep her in Sydney. He was well aware that all her hostility was because she believed otherwise. And for two years he had let her think the worst, mainly because she had refused to listen to anything he had to say. It was apparent now that she was still refusing to listen.

"Have you finished talking, Micah?"

Her question brought his attention back to the present. "No, not by a long shot. But I can't say it all tonight. I need to see you tomorrow. I know you'll be in town for the next couple of days and so will I. Let's do lunch. Even better, let's spend that time together to clear things up between us."

"Clear things up between us?" Kalina sneered in an angry whisper as red-hot fury tore through her. She was convinced that Micah had lost his ever-loving mind. Did he honestly think she would want to spend a single minute in his presence? Even being here now with him was stretching her to the limit. Where was a good glass of champagne when she wanted it? Nothing would make her happier right now than to toss a whole freakin' glass full in his face.

"I think I need to explain a few things to you, Micah. There's really nothing to clear up. Evidently you think I'm a woman that a man can treat any kind of way. Well, I have news for you. I won't take it. I don't need you any more than you need me. I don't appreciate the way you and Dad manipulated things to satisfy your need to exert some kind of power over me. And I—"

"Power? Do you think that's what I was trying to do, Kalina? Exert some kind of *power* over you? Just what kind of person do you honestly think I am?"

She ignored the tinge of disappointment she heard in his voice. It was probably just an act anyway. At the end of those two months, she'd discovered just what a great actor Micah could be. When she'd found out the truth, she had dubbed him the great pretender.

Kalina lifted her chin and straightened her spine. "I think you are just like all the other men my father tried throwing at me. He says jump and you all say how high. I thought you were different and was proven wrong. You see Dad as some sort of military hero, a legend, and whatever he says is gospel. And although Micah is a book in the Bible, last time I checked, my father's name was not. I am twenty-seven and old enough to make my own decisions about what I want to do and where I want to go. And neither you nor my father have anything to say about it. Furthermore—"

The next thing she knew, she was swept off her feet and into Micah's arms. His mouth came down hard, snatching air from her lungs and whatever words she was about to say from her lips.

She struggled against him, but only for a minute. That was all the time it took for those blasted memories of how good he tasted and just how well he kissed to come crashing over her, destroying her last shred of resistance. And then she settled down and gave in to what she knew had to be pleasure of the most intense kind.

God, he had missed this, Micah thought, pulling Kalina closer into his embrace while plundering her mouth with an intensity he felt in every part of his body. She had started shooting off her mouth, accusing him of things he hadn't done. Suddenly, he'd been filled with an overwhelming urge to kiss her mouth shut. So he had.

And with the kiss came memories of how things

had been between them their last time together, before anger had set in and destroyed their happiness. Had it really been two years since he'd tasted this, the most delectable tongue any woman could possess? And the body pressed against his was like none other. A perfect fit. The way she was returning the kiss was telling him she had missed this intimate connection as much as he had.

Her accusations bothered him immensely because there was no truth to what she'd said. He, of all people, was not—and never would be—a yes-man to her father, or to anyone. Her allegations showed just how little she knew him, and he intended to remedy that. But for now, he just wanted to enjoy this.

He deepened the kiss and felt the simmer sear his flesh, heat his skin and sizzle through to his bones. Then there was that surge of desire that flashed through his veins and set off a rumble of need in his chest. He'd found this kind of effect from mouth-to-mouth contact with a woman only happened with Kalina. She was building an ache within him, one only she had the ability to soothe.

Over the past two years he'd thought he was immune to this and to her, but the moment she had walked into the ballroom tonight, he'd known that Kalina was in his blood in a way no other woman could or would ever be. Even now, his heart was knocking against his ribs and he was inwardly chanting her name.

Lulled by the gentle breeze as well as the sweetness of her mouth, he wrapped his arms around her waist as something akin to molten liquid flowed over his senses. Damn, he was feeling the heat, and it was causing his pulse to quicken and his body to become aroused in a way it hadn't in years. Two years, to be exact.

And now he wanted to make up for lost time. How could she think he had pretended the passion that always flowed through his veins whenever he held her, kissed her or made love to her? He couldn't help tunneling his fingers through her hair. He'd noticed she was wearing it differently and liked the style on her. But there was very little about Kalina Daniels that he didn't like. All of which he found hard to resist.

He deepened the kiss even more when it was obvious she was just as taken, just as aroused and just as needy as he was. She could deny some things, but she couldn't deny this. Oh, she was mad at him and that was apparent. But it was also evident that all her anger had transformed to passion so thick that the need to make love to her was clawing at him, deep.

Conversation between an approaching couple had Kalina quickly pulling out of his arms. All it took was one look in her eyes beneath the softly lit lanterns to see the kiss had fired her up.

He leaned in, bringing his lips close to hers. "You are wrong about me, Kal. I never sold out to your father. I'm my own man. No one tells me what to do. If you believe otherwise, then you don't really know me."

He saw something flicker in her eyes. He also felt the tension surrounding them, the charged atmosphere, the electrified tingle making its way up his spine. Now more than ever, he was fully aware of her. Her scent. Her looks.

She was breathtaking in the sexy, one-shoulder, black cocktail dress that hugged her curves better than any race car could hug the curves at Indy. There was a sensuality about her that would make any man's pulse rise. Other men had been leery of approaching her that night in D.C. when he'd first flirted with her. After all, she was General Daniels's daughter and it was a known fact the man had placed her on a pedestal. But unlike the other men, Micah wasn't military under her father's command. He was civilian personnel who didn't have to take orders from the general.

She surprised him out of his thoughts when she leaned forward. He reached out for her only to have his hands knocked out of the way. The eyes staring at him were again flaring in anger. "I'm only going to say this once more, Micah. Stay away from me. I don't want to have anything else to do with you," she hissed, her breath fanning across his lips.

He sighed heavily. "Obviously you weren't listening, Kalina. I didn't have an affair with you because your father ordered me to. I was with you because I wanted to be. And you're going to have a hard time convincing me that you can still be upset with me after having shared a kiss like that."

"Think what you want. It doesn't matter anymore, Micah."

He intended to make it matter. "Spend tomorrow with me. Give it some thought."

"There's nothing to think about. Go use someone else."

Anger flashed through him. "I didn't use you." And then in a low husky tone, he added, "You meant a lot to me, Kalina."

Kalina swallowed. There was a time when she would have given anything to hear him say that. Even now, she wished that she could believe him, but she could not forget the look of guilt on his face when she'd stumbled across him discussing her with her father. She had stood in the shadows and listened. It hadn't been hard to put two and two together. She had fled from the party, caught a cab and returned to the hotel where she quickly packed her stuff and checked out.

Her father had been the first one she'd confronted, and he'd told her everything. How he had talked Micah into doing whatever it took to keep her in Sydney and away from Beijing. Her father claimed he'd done it for her own good, but he hadn't thought Micah would go so far as to seduce her. An affair hadn't been in their plan.

"You don't believe you meant something to me," he said again when she stood there and said nothing.

She lifted her chin. "No, I don't believe you. How can I think I meant anything to you other than a good time in bed when you explicitly told me in the very beginning that what we were sharing was a no-strings affair? And other than in the bedroom, you'd never let me get close to you. There's so much about you I don't know. Like your family, for instance. So how can you expect me to believe that I meant anything to you, Micah?"

Then, without saying another word, she turned and walked back toward the ballroom. She hoped that would be the end of it. Micah had hurt her once, and she would not let him do so again.

Two

By the time Micah got to his hotel room he was madder than hell. He slammed the door behind him. When he had returned to the ballroom, Kalina was nowhere to be found. Considering his present mood, that had been a good thing.

Now he moved across the room to toss his car keys on a table while grinding his teeth together. If she thought she'd seen the last of him then he had news for her. She was sadly mistaken. There was no way he would let her wash him off. No way and no how.

That kiss they'd shared had pretty much sealed things, whether she admitted it or not. He had not only felt her passion, he'd tasted it. She was still upset with him, but that hadn't stopped them from arousing each other. After the kiss, there had been fire in her eyes. However, the fire hadn't just come from her anger.

He stopped at a window and looked out, breathing heavily from the anger consuming him. Even at this hour the nation's capital was busy, if the number of cars on the road was anything to go by. But he didn't want to think about what anyone else was doing at the moment.

Micah rubbed his hand down his face. Okay, so Kalina had told the truth about him not letting her get too close. Thanks to an affair he'd had while in college, he'd been cautious. As a student, he'd fallen in love with a woman only to find out she'd been sleeping with one of her professors to get a better grade. The crazy thing about the situation was that she'd honestly thought he should understand and forgive her for what she'd done. He hadn't and had made up in his mind not to let another woman get close again. He hadn't shared himself emotionally with another woman since then.

But during his affair with Kalina, he had begun to let his guard down. How could she not know when their relationship had begun to change from a strictly no-strings affair to something more? Granted, there hadn't been any time for candlelight dinners, strolls in the park, flowers and such, but he had shared more with her than he had with any other woman…in the bedroom.

He drew in a deep breath and had to ask himself, "But what about outside the bedroom, man? Did you give her reason to think of anything beyond that?" He knew the answer immediately.

No, he hadn't. And she was right, he hadn't told her anything about his family and he knew why. He'd taken his college lover, Patrice, home and introduced her to the family as the woman he would one day marry. The woman who would one day have his children. She had gotten close to them. They had liked her and in the end she had betrayed them as much as she had betrayed him.

He lifted his head to stare up at the ceiling. Now he could see all his mistakes, and the first of many was letting two years go by without seeking out Kalina. He'd been well aware of what her father had told her. But he'd assumed she would eventually think things through and realize her dad hadn't been completely truthful with her. Instead, she had believed the worst. Mainly because she truly hadn't known Micah.

His BlackBerry suddenly went off. He pulled it out of his pocket and saw it was a call from home. His oldest brother, Dillon. There was only a two-year difference in their ages, and they'd always been close. Any other time he would have been excited about receiving a call from home, but not now and not tonight. However, Dillon was family, so Micah answered the call.

"Hello?"

"We haven't heard from you in a while, and I thought I would check in," Dillon said.

Micah leaned back against the wall. Because Dillon was the oldest, he had pretty much taken over things when their parents, aunt and uncle had died in a plane crash. There had been fifteen Westmorelands—nine of them under the age of sixteen—and Dillon had vowed to keep everyone together. And he had.

Micah had been in his second year of college and hadn't been around to give Dillon a hand. But Ramsey, their cousin, who was just months younger than Dillon, had pitched in to help manage things.

"I'm fine," Micah heard himself saying when in all

honesty he was anything but. He drew in a deep breath and said, "I saw Kalina tonight."

Although Dillon had never met Kalina he knew who she was. One night while home, Micah had told Dillon all about her and what had happened to tear them apart. Dillon had suggested that he contact Kalina and straighten things out, as well as admit how he felt about her. But a stubborn streak wouldn't let Micah do so. Now he wished he would have acted on his brother's advice.

"And how is she?"

Micah rubbed another hand down his face. "She still hates my guts, if that's what you want to know. Go ahead and say I told you so."

"I wouldn't do that."

No, he wouldn't. That wasn't Dillon's style, although saying so would have been justified.

"So what are you going to do, Micah?"

Micah figured the only reason Dillon was asking was because his brother knew how much Kalina meant to him…even if *she* didn't know it. And her not knowing was no one's fault but his.

"Not sure what I'm going to do because no matter what I say, she won't believe me. A part of me just wants to say forget it, I don't need the hassle, but I can't, Dil. I just can't walk away from her."

"Then don't. You've never been a quitter. The Micah Westmoreland I know goes after what he wants and has never let anyone or anything stand in his way. But if you don't want her enough to fight for her and make her see the truth, then I don't know what to tell you."

Then, as if the subject of Kalina was a closed one, Dillon promptly began talking about something else. He told Micah how their sister-in-law, Bella, was coming along in her pregnancy, and that the doctors had verified twins, both girls.

"They're the first on our side," he said. Their parents had had all boys. Seven of them.

"I know, and everyone is excited and ready for her to be born," Dillon replied. "But I don't think anyone is as ready as Jason," he said of their brother and the expectant father.

The rest of the conversation was spent with Dillon bringing Micah up to date on what was going down on the home front. His brother Jason had settled into wedded bliss and so had his cousin Derringer. Micah shook his head. He could see Jason with a wife, but for the life of him, considering how Derringer used to play the field and enjoy it immensely, the thought of him settled down with one woman was still taking some getting used to. Dillon also mentioned that Ramsey and Chloe's son would be born in a few months.

"Do you think you'll be able to be here for li'l Callum's christening?"

Micah shook his head. Now, that was another one it was hard to believe had settled down. His cousin Gemma had a husband. She used to be a real pistol where men were concerned, but it seemed that Callum Austell had changed all that. She was now living in Australia with him and their two-month-old son.

"I plan to be there," Micah heard himself saying. "In a few weeks, I'll have thirty days to kill. I leave for Bajadad the day after tomorrow and I will be there for two weeks. I'll fly home from there." Bajadad was a small and beautiful city in northern India near the Himalayan foothills.

"It will be good seeing you again."

Micah couldn't help chuckling. "You make it sound like I haven't been home in years, Dil. I was just there seven months ago for Jason's wedding reception."

"I know, but anytime you come home and we can get everyone together is good."

Micah nodded. He would agree to that, and for Gemma's baby's christening, all the Westmorelands would be there, including their cousins from Atlanta, Texas and Montana.

Moments later, Micah ended his phone conversation with Dillon. He headed for the bedroom to undress and take a shower. The question Dillon asked him rang through his head. What was he going to do about Kalina?

Just like that, he remembered the proposition she'd made to Major Rose. And as he'd told her, he had no intention of letting the man go anywhere with her.

And just how are you going to stop her? His mind taunted. *She doesn't want to have anything to do with you. Thanks to her daddy's lie, you lost her. Get over it.*

He drew in a deep breath, knowing that was the kicker. He couldn't get over it. Dillon was right. Micah was not a quitter, and it was about time he made Kalina aware of that very fact.

Micah was pulled from his thoughts when his cell phone rang again. Pulling it from his pants pocket, he saw it was an official call from the Department of Health and Human Services. "Yes, Major Harris?"

"Dr. Westmoreland, first I want to apologize for calling you so late. And secondly, I'm calling to report changes in the assignment to India."

"And what are the changes, Major?"

"You will leave tomorrow instead of Monday. And Dr. Moore's wife went into labor earlier today so he has to be pulled off the team. We're going to have to send in a replacement."

Micah headed the U.S. epidemic response team consisting of over thirty epidemiologists, so calling to let him know of any changes was the norm. "That's fine."

He was about to thank her for calling and hang up when she said, "Now I need to call Dr. Daniels. Unfortunately, her vacation has to be canceled so she can take Dr. Moore's place."

Micah's pulse rate shot up and there was a deep thumping in his chest, close to his heart. "What did you say?" he asked, to make sure he'd heard her correctly.

"I said Dr. Daniels will be Dr. Moore's replacement since she's next in line on the on-call list. Unfortunately, her vacation was supposed to start tomorrow."

"What a pity," he said, not really feeling such sympathy. What others would see as Kalina's misfortune, he saw as his blessing. This change couldn't be any better if he'd planned it himself, and he intended to make sure Kalina's canceled vacation worked to his advantage.

Of course, when she found out she would automatically think the worst. She would assume the schedule change was his idea and that he was responsible for ruining her vacation. But it wouldn't be the first time she'd falsely accused him of something.

"Good night, Dr. Westmoreland."

He couldn't help smiling, feeling as if he had a new lease on life. "Good night, Major Harris."

He clicked off the phone thinking someone upstairs

had to like him, and he definitely appreciated it. Now he would have to come up with a plan to make sure he didn't screw things up with Kalina this time.

Kalina paced her hotel room. *What was she going to do about Micah?*

She came to a stop long enough to touch her lips. She'd known letting him kiss her had been a bad move, but she hadn't been able to resist the feel of his mouth on hers. She should have been prepared for it. She'd seen the telltale signs in his eyes. He hadn't taken her off to a secluded place to talk about the weather. She'd been prepared for them to face off, have it out. And they'd done that. Then they'd ended up kissing each other senseless.

As much as she would like to do so, she couldn't place the blame solely at his feet. She had gone after his mouth just as greedily as he'd gone after hers. A rush of heat had consumed her the moment he'd stuck his tongue inside her mouth. So, okay, they were still attracted to each other. No big deal.

Kalina frowned. It *was* a big deal, especially when, even now, whirling sensations had taken over her stomach. She knew with absolute certainty that she didn't want to be attracted to Micah Westmoreland. She didn't want to have anything to do with him, period.

She glanced over at the clock and saw it was just past midnight. She was still wearing her cocktail dress, since she hadn't changed out of her clothes. She had begun pacing the moment she'd returned to her hotel room. Why was she letting him do this to her? And why was he lying, claiming he had not been in cahoots with her father when she knew differently?

Moving to the sofa, she sat down, still not ready to get undressed, because once she got in bed all she would do was dream about Micah. She leaned back in her seat, remembering the first time they'd worked together. She had arrived in Sydney, and he had been the one to pick her up from the airport. They had met a year earlier and their attraction to each other had been hot and instantaneous. It had taken less than five minutes in his presence that day to see that the heat hadn't waned any.

She would give them both credit for trying to ignore it. After all, they'd had an important job to do. And they'd made it through the first week, managing to keep their hands off each other. But the beginning of the next week had been the end of that. It had happened when they'd worked late one night, sorting out samples, dissecting birds, trying to make sure the bird flu didn't spread to the continent of Australia.

Technically, he had been her boss, since he headed the government's epidemic response team. But he'd never exerted the power of that position over her or anyone. He had treated everyone as a vital and important part of the team. Micah was a born leader and everyone easily gave him the respect he deserved.

And on that particular night, she'd given him something else. He had walked her to her hotel room, and she had invited him in. It hadn't been a smart move, but she had gotten tired of playing games. Tired of lusting after him and trying to keep her distance. They were adults and that night she'd figured they deserved to finally let go and do what adults did when they had the hots for each other.

Until that night, she'd thought the whole sex act was

overrated. Micah had proven her wrong so many times that first night that she still got a tingling sensation just remembering it. She'd assumed it was a one night-stand, but that hadn't been the case. He had invited her out to dinner the following night and provided her with the terms of a no-strings affair, if she was interested. She had been more than interested. She was dedicated to her career and hadn't wanted to get involved in a serious relationship any more than he did.

That night they had reached a mutual agreement, and from then on they'd been exclusively involved during the two months they'd remained in Sydney. She was so content with their affair that when her earlier request for an assignment to Beijing had been denied, it really hadn't bothered her.

That contentment had lasted until she'd returned to the States and discovered the truth. Not only had her father manipulated her orders, but he'd solicited Micah's help in doing whatever he had to do to make sure she was kept happy in Sydney. She had been the one left looking like a complete fool, and she doubted she would forgive either of them for what they'd done.

Thinking she'd had enough of strolling down memory lane where the hurt was too much to bear, Kalina got up from the sofa and was headed toward the bedroom to change and finally attempt to sleep, when her cell phone rang. She picked it up off the table and saw it was Major Sally Harris, the administrative coordinator responsible for Kalina's assignments. She wondered why the woman would be calling her so late at night.

Kalina flipped on the phone. "Yes, Major Harris?"

"Dr. Daniels, I regret calling you so late and I want to apologize, because I have to deliver bad news."

Kalina frowned. "And what bad news is that?"

"Dr. Moore's wife went into labor earlier today so he has to be pulled off the epidemic response team headed out for Bajadad. I know your vacation was to start tomorrow, but we need your assistance in India."

Kalina drew in a deep breath. Although she hadn't made any definite vacation plans, she had looked forward to taking time off. "How long will I be needed in Bajadad?"

"For two weeks, beginning tomorrow, and then you can resume your vacation."

She nodded. There was no need to ask if there was someone else they could call since she knew the answer to that already. The epidemic response team had thinned out over the past few years with a war going on. And since the enemy liked to engage in chemical warfare, a number of epidemiologists had been sent to work in Afghanistan and Iraq.

"Dr. Daniels?"

Resigned, she said. "Yes, of course." Not that she had a choice in the matter. She was civilian, but orders from her boss were still meant to be followed, and she couldn't rightly get mad at Jess Moore because his wife was having a baby. "I'll be ready to head out tomorrow."

"Thanks. I'll send your information to your email address," Major Harris said.

"That will be fine."

"And Dr. Westmoreland has been notified of the change in personnel."

Kalina almost dropped the phone. "Dr. Westmoreland?"

"Yes?"

She frowned. "Why was he notified?"

"Because he's the one heading up the team."

Kalina's head began spinning. No one would be so cruel as to make her work with Micah again. She drew in a deep breath when a suspicion flowed through her mind. "Was Dr. Westmoreland the one to suggest that I replace Dr. Moore?"

"No, the reason you were called is that you're the next doctor on the on-call list."

Lucky me. Kalina shook her head, feeling anything but lucky. The thought of spending two weeks around Micah had her fuming inside. And regardless of what Major Harris said, it was hard to believe it was merely a coincidence that she was next on the call list. Micah was well liked and she knew all about his numerous connections and contacts. If she found out he had something to do with this change then…

"Dr. Daniels?"

"Yes?"

"Is there anything else you'd like to know?"

"No, there's nothing else."

"Thank you, Dr. Daniels, and good night."

"Good night, Major Harris."

Kalina hung up the phone knowing she couldn't let her feelings for Micah interfere with her work. She had a job to do, and she intended to do it. She would just keep her distance from him. She went into the bedroom and began tugging off her clothes as she became lost in a mix of disturbing thoughts.

The first thing she would do would be to set ground rules between her and Micah. If he saw this as a golden opportunity to get back in her bed then he was sadly mistaken. She was not the type of woman to forgive easily. Just as she'd told him earlier tonight, there was nothing else they had to say to each other regarding what happened between them two years ago. It was over and done with.

But if that kiss was anything to go by, she would need to be on guard around him at all times. Because their relationship might be over and done with, but the attraction between them was still alive and well.

Three

Micah saw the fire in Kalina's eyes from ten feet away. She glared as she moved toward him, chin up and spine stiff. She meant business. He slid a hand into the pocket of his jeans, thinking that he was glad it was Sunday and there were few people around. It seemed they were about to have it out once again.

This morning, upon awakening, he had decided the best way to handle her was to let her assume he wasn't handling her at all, to make her think that he had accepted her decision about how things would be between them. And when he felt the time was right, he would seize every opportunity he could get and let her know in no uncertain terms that her decision hadn't been his.

His gaze swept over her now. She was dressed for travel, with her hair pulled back in a ponytail and a pair of comfortable shoes on her feet. She looked good in her jeans and tank top and lightweight jacket. But then, she looked better than any woman he knew, in clothes or out of them.

He continued to stare at her while remembering her body stretched out beneath his when he'd made love to her. Even now, he could recall how it felt to skim his hands down the front of her body, tangle his fingers in her womanly essence while kissing her with a degree of passion he hadn't been aware of until her.

His heart began racing, and he could feel the zipper of his pants getting tight. He withdrew his hands from his pockets. The last thing he needed was for her to take note of his aroused state, so he turned and entered the private office he used whenever he was in D.C. on business. Besides, he figured the best place to have the encounter he knew was coming was behind closed doors.

By the time she had entered the office, all but slamming the door behind her, he was standing behind the desk.

He met her gaze, and felt the anger she wasn't trying to hide. As much as he wanted to cross the room and pull her into his arms and kiss her, convince her how wrong she was about him, common sense dictated he stay put. He intended to do what he hadn't done two years ago. Give her the chance to get to know him. He was convinced if she'd truly known him, she would not have been so quick to believe the worst about him.

"Dr. Daniels, I take it you're ready to fly out to Bajadad."

Her gaze narrowed. "And you want me to believe you had nothing to do with those orders, Micah?"

He crossed his arms over his chest and met her stare head-on. "At this point, Kalina, you can believe whatever you like. For me to deny it wouldn't matter since you wouldn't believe me anyway."

"And why should I?" she snapped.

"Because I have no reason to lie," he said simply. "Have you ever considered the possibility that I could be telling the truth? Just in case you need to hear it from me—just like I had nothing to do with your father's plan to keep you out of Beijing, your orders to go to Bajadad were not my idea. Although I embrace the schedule change wholeheartedly. You're a good doctor, and I can't think of anyone I want more on my team. We're dealing with a suspicious virus. Five people have died already and the government suspects it might be part of something we need to nip in the bud as soon as possible. However, we won't know what we're dealing with until we get there."

He watched as her whole demeanor changed in the wake of the information he had just provided. Her stiffened spine relaxed and her features became alert. No matter what, she was a professional, and as he'd said, she was good at what she did.

"What's the point of entry?" she asked, moving to stand in front of the desk.

"So far, only by ingestion. It's been suspected that something was put in the water supply. If that's true, it will be up to us to find out what it is."

She nodded, and he knew she completely understood. The government's position was that if the enemy had developed some kind of deadly chemical then the United States needed to know about it. It was important to determine early on what they were up against and how they could protect U.S. military personnel.

"And how was it detected, Micah?" she was calm

and relaxed as she questioned him. He moved to sit on the edge of his desk. Not far from where she stood. He wondered if she'd taken note of their proximity.

He wished she wasn't wearing his favorite perfume and that he didn't remember just how dark her eyes would become in the heat of passion. Kalina Daniels was an innately sensuous woman. There was no doubt about it.

"Five otherwise healthy adults over the age of fifty were found dead within the same week with no obvious signs of trauma," he heard himself saying. "However, their tongues had enlarged to twice the normal size. Other than that, there was nothing else, not even evidence of a foreign substance in their bloodstream."

He saw the look in her eyes while she was digesting what he'd said. Most terrorist groups experimented on a small number of people before unleashing anything in full force, just to make sure their chemical warfare weapon was effective. It was too early to make an assumption about what they would be facing, but the researcher who was already there waiting on them had stated his suspicions. Before 9/11 chemical weapons were considered a poor man's atomic bomb. However, because of their ability to reach millions of people in so many different ways, these weapons were now considered the worst and most highly effective of all forms of warfare.

"Have you ever been to Bajadad?" she asked him.

He met her gaze. "Yes, several years ago, right after the first democratic elections were held. It was my first assignment after leaving college and coming to work for the federal government. We were sent there on a peace-finding mission when members of the king's household had become ill. Some suspected foul play. However, it didn't take us long to determine it hadn't been all that serious, just a contaminated sack of wheat that should never have been used."

He could tell by the look in her eyes that she'd become intrigued. That's how it had always been with her. She would ask a lot of questions to quench that curiosity of hers. She thought he'd lived an adventurous life as an epidemiologist, while, thanks to her father, she'd been deliberately kept on the sidelines.

In a way, he was surprised she was going to Bajadad. Either the old man had finally learned his lesson or he was getting lax in keeping up with his daughter's whereabouts. He knew her father had worked behind the scenes, wielding power, influencing his contacts, to make sure Kalina had assignments only in the States or in first-world countries. He'd discovered, after the fact, that her time in Sydney had been orchestrated to keep her out of Beijing without giving her a reason to get suspicious.

Micah stood and decided to shift topics. He met Kalina's gaze when he said, "I think we need to talk about last night."

He watched her spine stiffen as she once again shifted into a defensive mode. "No, we don't."

"Yes, we do Kalina. We're going out on a mission together, and I think it's going to be important that we're comfortable around each other and put our personal differences aside. I'd be the first to admit I've made a lot of mistakes where you're concerned, and I regret making them. Now you believe the worst of me and nothing I can say or do will change that."

He paused a moment, knowing he had to chose his

words carefully. "You don't have to worry about me mixing business with pleasure, because I refuse to become involved with a woman who doesn't trust me. So there can never be anything between us again."

There, he'd said it. He tasted the lie on his tongue, but knew his reasons for his concocted statement were justified. He had no intention of giving her up. Ever. But she had to learn to trust him. And he would do whatever he had to do to make that happen.

Although she tried to shelter her reaction, he'd seen how his words had jolted her body. There was no doubt in his mind she had felt the depth of what he'd said. A part of him wanted to believe that deep down she still cared for him.

She lifted her chin in a stubborn frown. "Good. I'm glad we got that out of the way and that we understand each other."

He glanced down at his watch. "Our flight leaves in a few hours. I would offer you a ride to the airport, but I'm catching a ride with someone myself."

She tilted her head back and looked at him. "No problem. I reserved a rental car."

Kalina looked at her own watch and slipped the straps of her purse onto her shoulders. "I need to be going."

"I'll walk out with you," he said, falling into step beside her. He had no problem offering her a ride if she needed one, but he hadn't wanted to appear too anxious to be in her company. "We're looking at a twelve-hour flight. I'd advise you to eat well before we fly out. The food we're going to be served on the plane won't be the best."

She chuckled and the sound did something to him. It felt good to be walking beside her. "Don't think I don't know about military-airplane food. I'm going to stop and grab me a sandwich from Po'Boys," she said.

He knew she regretted mentioning the restaurant when he glanced over and saw the blush on her face. Chances were, like him, she was remembering the last time they'd gone there together. It had been their first night back in the States after Australia. He might not recall what all they'd eaten that night, but he did remember everything they'd done in the hotel room afterward.

"Whatever you get, eat enough for the both of us," he said, breaking the silence between them.

She glanced over at him. "I will."

They were now outside, standing on the top steps of the Centers for Disease Control. "Well, I guess I'll be seeing you on the flight. Take care until then, Kal."

Then, without looking back, he moved to the car that pulled up to the curb at that very moment. He smiled, thinking the timing was perfect when he saw who was driving the car.

He glanced up at the sky. He had a feeling someone up there was definitely on his side. His cousin, Senator Reggie Westmoreland, had called him that morning, inviting him to lunch. Reggie, his wife, Olivia, and their one-year-old twin sons made Washington their home for part of the year. It was Olivia and not Reggie who'd come to pick him up to take him to their house in Georgetown. She was a beautiful woman, and he could just imagine the thoughts going through Kalina's mind right now.

* * *

Kalina stood and watched Micah stroll down the steps toward the waiting car. He looked good in a chambray shirt that showed the width of his broad shoulders and jeans that hugged his masculine thighs, making her appreciate what a fine specimen of a man he was.

He worked out regularly and it showed. No matter from what angle you saw him—front, back or side— one looked just as good as the other. And from the side-glances of several women who were climbing the steps and passing by him as he moved down, she was reminded again that she wasn't the only one who appreciated that fact.

Oh, why did he have to call her Kal? It was the nickname he'd given her during their affair. No one else called her that. Her father detested nicknames and always referred to her by her first and middle name. To her dad she was Kalina Marie.

She tried not to show any emotion as she watched a woman get out of the car, smiling brightly while moving toward Micah. She was almost in his face by the time his foot touched the last step, and he gave the woman a huge hug and a warm smile as if he was happy to see her, as well.

No wonder he's so quick to write you off, she thought in exasperated disgust, hating that seeing Micah with another woman bothered her. *He's already involved with someone else. Well, what did you expect? It's been two years. Just because you haven't been in a serious relationship since then doesn't mean he hasn't. And besides, you're the one who called things off. Accused him of being in league with your father...*

Kalina shook her head as the car, with Micah in it,

pulled off. Why was she trying to rehash anything? She knew the truth, and no matter how strenuously Micah claimed otherwise, she believed her father. Yes, he was controlling, but he loved her. He had no reason to lie. He had confessed his part and had admitted to his involvement in Micah's part, as well. So why couldn't Micah just come clean and fess up? And why had she felt a bout of jealousy when he'd hugged that woman? Why did she care that the woman was jaw-droppingly beautiful, simply gorgeous with not a hair on her head out of place?

Tightening her hand on her purse, Kalina walked down the steps toward the parking lot. She had to get a grip on more than her purse. She needed to be in complete control of her senses while dealing with Micah.

"Sorry to impose, but I think this is the only seat left on the plane," Micah said as he slid into the empty seat next to Kalina.

Her eyes had been closed as she waited for take-off, but she immediately opened them, looking at him strangely before lifting up slightly to glance around, as if to make sure he was telling the truth.

He smiled as be buckled his seat belt. "You need to stop doing that, you know."

She arched an eyebrow. "Doing what?"

"Acting like everything coming out of my mouth is a lie."

She shrugged what he knew were beautiful shoulders. "Well, once you tell one lie, people have a tendency not to believe you in the future. Sort of like the boy who cried wolf." She then closed her eyes again as if to dismiss him.

He didn't plan to let her response be the end of it. "What's going to happen when you find out you've been wrong about me?"

She opened her eyes and glanced over at him, looking as if the thought of her being wrong was not even a possibility. "Not that I think that will happen, but if it does then I'll owe you an apology."

"And when it does happen I might just be reluctant to accept your apology." He then leaned back in his seat and closed his eyes, this time dismissing her and leaving her with something to chew on.

The flight attendant prevented further conversation between them when she came on the intercom to provide flight rules and regulations. He kept his eyes closed. Kalina's insistence that he would conspire with her father grated on a raw nerve each and every time she said it.

Moments later, he felt the movement of the plane glide down the runway before tilting as it eased into the clouds. Over the years, he'd gotten used to air travel, but that didn't mean he particularly liked it. All he had to do was recall that he had lost four vital members of his family in a plane crash. And he couldn't help remembering that tragic and deep-felt loss each and every time he boarded a plane, even after all these years.

"She's pretty."

He opened his eyes and glanced over at Kalina. "Who is?"

"That woman who picked you up from the CDC today."

He nodded. "Thanks. I happen to think she's pretty, too," he said honestly. In fact, he thought all his cousins and brothers had married beautiful women. Not only were they beautiful, they were smart, intelligent and strong.

"Have the two of you been seeing each other long?"

It would be real simple to tell her that Olivia was a relative, but he decided to let her think whatever she wanted. "No, and we really aren't seeing each other now. We're just friends," he said.

"Close friends?"

He closed his eyes again. "Yes." He had been tempted to keep his eyes open just to see her expression, but knew closing them would make his nonchalance more effective.

"How long have the two of you known each other?"

He knew she was trying to figure out if Olivia had come before or after her. "Close to five years now."

"Oh."

So far everything he'd said had been the truth. He just wasn't elaborating. It was his choice and his right. Besides, he was giving her something to think about.

Deciding she'd asked enough questions about Olivia, he said, "You might want to rest awhile. We have a long flight ahead of us."

And he intended on sharing every single hour of it with her. It wasn't a coincidence that the last seat on the military jet had been next to her and that he'd taken it. There hadn't been any assigned seats on this flight. Passengers could sit anywhere, and, with the help of the flight attendant, he'd made sure they had sat everywhere but next to Kalina. The woman just happened to know that *New York Times* bestselling author Rock Mason, aka Stone Westmoreland, was Micah's cousin. The woman was a huge fan and the promise of an autographed copy of Stone's next action thriller had gone a long way.

Micah kept his eyes closed but could still inhale Kalina's scent. He could envision her that morning, dabbing cologne all over her body, a body he'd had intimate knowledge of for two wonderful months. He was convinced he knew where every mole was located, and he was well acquainted with that star-shaped scar near her hip bone that had come as a result of her taking a tumble off a skateboard at the age of twelve.

He drew in a deep breath, taking in her scent one more time for good measure. For now, he needed to pretend he was ignoring her. Sitting here lusting after Kalina wasn't doing him any good and was just weakening his resolve to keep her at a distance while he let her get to know him. He couldn't let that happen. But he couldn't help it when he opened his eyes, turned to her and said, "Oh, by the way, Kalina. You still have the cutest dimples." He then turned to face straight ahead before closing his eyes once again.

Satisfied he might have soothed her somewhat, he stretched his long legs out in front of him, at least as far as they could go, and tilted his seat back. He might as well get as comfortable as he could for the long flight.

He'd been given a good hand to play and he planned on making the kind of win that the gambler in the family, his cousin Ian, would be proud of. The stakes were high, but Micah intended to be victorious.

So Micah had known the woman during their affair. Did that mean he'd taken back up with her after their time together had ended? Kalina wondered. He said he and the woman were only friends, but she'd known men to claim only friendship even while sleeping with a woman every night. Men tended not to place the same importance on an affair as women did. She, of all people, should know that.

And how dare he compliment her on her dimples at a time like this and in the mood she was in. She had to work with him, but she was convinced she didn't even like him anymore. Yet in all fairness, she shouldn't be surprised by the comment about her dimples. He'd told her numerous times that her dimples were the first thing he'd noticed about her. They were permanent fixtures on her face, whether she smiled or not.

And then there was the way he'd looked at her when he'd said it. Out of the clear blue sky, he had turned those gorgeous bedroom-brown eyes on her and remarked on her dimples. Her stomach had clenched. It had been so unexpected it had sent her world tilting for a minute. And before she'd recovered, he'd turned back around and closed his eyes.

Now he was reclining comfortably beside her. All man. All sexy. All Westmoreland. And seemingly all bored…at least with her. She had a good mind to wake him up and engage in some conversation just for the hell of it, but then she thought better of it. Micah Westmoreland was a complex man and just thinking about how complex he could be had tension building at her temples.

She couldn't help thinking about all the things she didn't know about him. For some reason, he'd never shared much about himself or his family. She knew he had several brothers, but that fact was something she'd discovered by accident and not because he'd told her about them. She'd just so happened to overhear a conversation between him and his good friend Dr. Beau Smallwood. And she did know his parents had died in a plane crash when he was in college. He'd only told her that because she'd asked.

Her life with her military father was basically an open book. After her mother had died of cervical cancer when Kalina was ten, her father had pretty much clung to her like a vine. The only time they were separated was when he'd been called for active duty or another assignment where she wasn't allowed. Those were the days she spent on her grandparents' farm in Alabama. Joe and Claudia Daniels had passed away years ago, but Kalina still had fond memories of the time she'd spent with them.

Kalina glanced over at Micah again. It felt strange casually sitting next to a man who'd been inside her body…numerous times. A man whose tongue had licked her in places that made her blush to think about. Someone who had taken her probably in every position known to the average man and in some he'd probably created himself. He was the type of man a woman fantasized about. A shiver raced through her body just thinking about being naked with him.

Up to now, she had come to terms with the fact that she'd be working with Micah again, especially after what he'd said in his office earlier that morning. He didn't want to become involved with her, just as she didn't want to become involved with him. So why was she tempted to reach out and trace the line of his chin with her fingers or use the tip of her tongue to glisten his lips?

Oh, by the way, you still have the cutest dimples. If those words had been meant to get next to her, they had. And she wished they hadn't. She didn't want to remember anything about the last time they were together or what sharing those two months with him had meant to her.

And she especially did not want to remember what the man had meant to her.

Having no interest in the movie currently being shown and wanting to get her mind off the man next to her, she decided to follow Micah's lead. She tilted her seat back, closed her eyes and went to sleep.

Four

Micah awakened the next morning and stretched as he glanced around his bedroom. He'd been too tired when he'd arrived at the private villa last night to take note of his surroundings, but now he couldn't help smiling. He would definitely like it here. Kalina's room was right next door to his.

He slid out of bed and headed for the bathroom, thinking the sooner he got downstairs the better. The government had set up a lab for them in the basement of the villa and, according to the report he'd read, it would be fully equipped for their needs.

Twelve hours on a plane hadn't been an ideal way to spend time with Kalina, but he had managed to retain his cool. He'd even gone so far as to engage in friendly conversation about work. Otherwise, like him, she'd slept most of the time. Once he'd found her watching some romantic movie. Another time she'd been reading a book on one of those eReaders.

A short while after waking, Micah had dressed and was headed downstairs for breakfast. The other doctor on the team had arrived last week and Micah was looking forward to seeing him again. Theodus Mitchell was a doctor he'd teamed with before, who did excellent work in the field of contagious diseases.

Micah opened his bedroom door and walked out into the hallway the same time Kalina did. He smiled when he saw her, although he could tell by her expression that she wasn't happy to see him. "Kalina. Good morning."

"Good morning, Micah. You're going down for breakfast?"

"Yes, what about you?" he asked, falling into step beside her.

"Yes, although I'm not all that hungry," she said.

He definitely was, and it wasn't all food that had him feeling hungry. She looked good. Well rested. Sexy as hell in a pair of brown slacks and a green blouse. And she'd gotten rid of the ponytail. She was wearing her hair down to her shoulders. The style made her features appear even more beautiful.

"Well, I'm starving," he said as they stepped onto the elevator. "And I'm also anxious to get to the lab to see what we're up against. Did you get a chance to read the report?"

She nodded as the elevator door shut behind them. "Yes, I read it before going to bed. I wasn't all that sleepy."

They were the only ones in the elevator and suddenly memories flooded his brain. The last time they had been in an elevator alone she had tempted him so much that he had ended up taking her against a wall in one hell of a quickie. Thoughts of that time fired his blood.

Now, she had moved to stand at the far side of the elevator. She was staring into space, looking as if she didn't have a care in the world. He wanted to fire her blood the way she was firing his.

The elevator stopped on the first floor and as soon as the doors swooshed open, she was out. He couldn't help chuckling to himself as he followed her, thinking she was trying to put distance between them. Evidently, although she'd pretended otherwise, she had remembered their last time in an elevator together, as well.

A buffet breakfast was set up on the patio, and the moment he walked out onto the terrace, his glance was caught by the panoramic view of the Himalayas, looming high toward a beautiful April sky.

"Theo!"

"Kalina, good seeing you again."

He turned and watched Theo and Kalina embrace, not feeling the least threatened since everyone knew just how devoted Theo was to his beautiful wife, Renee, who was an international model. Inhaling the richness of the mountain air, Micah strolled toward the pair. The last time the three of them had teamed up together on an assignment had been in Sydney. Beau had also been part of their team.

Theo released Kalina and turned to Micah and smiled. "Micah, it's good seeing you, as well. It's like old times," Theo said with a hearty handshake.

Micah wondered if Theo assumed the affair with Kalina was still ongoing since he'd been there with them in Australia when it had started. "Yes, and from what I understand we're going to be busy for the next two weeks."

Theo nodded and a serious expression appeared on his face. "So far there haven't been any more deaths and that's a good thing."

Micah agreed. "The three of us can discuss it over breakfast."

Kalina sat beside Micah and tried to unravel her tangled thoughts. But there was nothing she could do with the heat that was rushing through her at that moment. There was no way she could put a lid on it. The desire flowing within her was too thick to confine. For some reason, even amidst the conversations going on—mostly between Micah and Theo—she couldn't stop her mind from drifting and grabbing hold of memories of what she and Micah had once shared.

"So what do you think, Kalina?"

She glanced over at Micah. Had he suspected her of daydreaming when she should have been paying attention? Both men had worked as epidemiologists for a lot longer than she had and had seen and done a lot more. She had enjoyed just sitting and listening to how they analyzed things, figuring she could learn a lot from them.

Micah, Theo and another epidemiologist by the name of Beau Smallwood had begun work for the federal government right out of medical school and were good friends; especially Beau and Micah who were the best of friends.

"I think, although we can't make assumptions until we have the data to support it, I agree that the deaths are suspicious."

Micah smiled, and she tried downplaying the effect that smile had on her. She had to remind herself that smile or no smile, he was someone who couldn't be trusted. Someone who had betrayed her.

"Well, then, I think we'd better head over to the lab to find out what we're up against,' Micah said, standing.

He reached for her tray and she pulled it back. "Thanks, but I can dispense with my own trash."

He nodded. "Suit yourself."

She stood and turned to walk off, but not before hearing Theo whisper to Micah, "Um, my friend, it sounds like there's trouble in paradise."

She was tempted to turn and alert Theo to the fact that "paradise" for them ended two years ago. Shaking off the anger she felt when she thought about that time in her life and the hurt she'd felt, she continued walking toward the trash can. She'd known at the start of her affair with Micah that it would be a short-term affair. He'd made certain she understood there were no strings, and she had.

But what she couldn't accept was knowing the entire thing had been orchestrated by her controlling father. The only reason she was here in India now was because the general was probably too busy with the war in Afghanistan to check up on her whereabouts. He probably felt pretty confident she was on vacation or assigned to some cushy job in the States. Although he claimed otherwise, she knew he was the reason she hadn't been given any hard-hitting assignments. If it hadn't been for Dr. Moore's baby, chances are she wouldn't be here now.

She was about to turn, when Micah came up beside

her to toss out his own trash. "Stop being so uptight with me, Kalina."

She glanced over at him and drew in a deep breath to keep from saying something that was totally rude. Instead, she met his gaze and said, "My being uptight, Micah, should be the least of your worries." She then walked off.

Micah watched her go, admiring the sway of her hips with every step she took. His feelings for Kalina were a lot more than sexual, but he was a man, and the woman had a body that any man would appreciate.

"I see she still doesn't know how you feel about her, Micah."

Micah glanced over and saw the humor in Theo's blue gaze. There was no reason to pretend he didn't know what the man was talking about. "No, she doesn't know."

"Then don't you think you ought to tell her?"

Micah chuckled. "With Kalina it won't be that easy. I need to show her rather than tell her because she doesn't believe anything I say."

"Ouch. Sounds like you have your work cut out for you then."

Micah nodded. "I do, but in the end it will be worth it."

Kalina was fully aware of the moment Micah entered the lab. With her eyes glued to the microscope, she hadn't looked up, but she knew without a doubt he was there and that he had looked her way. It was their first full day in Bajadad, and it had taken all her control to fight the attraction, the pull, the heat between them. She had played the part of the professional and had, hopefully, pulled it off. At least she believed Theo hadn't picked up on anything. He was too absorbed in the findings of today's lab reports to notice the air around them was charged.

But *she* had noticed. Not only had she picked up on the strong chemistry flowing between her and Micah, she had also picked up on his tough resistance. He would try to resist her as much as she would try to resist him, and she saw that as a good thing.

Even if they hadn't been involved two years ago, there was no way they would not be attracted to each other. He was a man and she was a woman, so quite naturally there would be a moment of awareness between them. Some things just couldn't be helped. But hopefully, by tomorrow, that awareness would have passed and they would be able to get down to the business they were sent here to carry out.

What if it didn't pass?

A funny feeling settled in her stomach at the thought of that happening. But all it took was the reminder of how he had betrayed her in the worst possible way to keep any attraction between them from igniting into full-blown passion.

However, she felt the need to remind herself that her best efforts hadn't drummed up any opposition to him when they'd been alone in the lab earlier that day. He had stood close while she'd gone over the reports, and she'd inhaled his scent while all kinds of conflicting emotions rammed through her. And every time she glanced up into his too-handsome face and stared into his turn-you-on brown eyes she could barely think straight.

Okay, she was faced with a challenge, but it wouldn't

be the first time nor did she figure it would be the last. She'd never been a person who was quick to jump into bed with a man just for the sake of doing so, and she had surprised herself with how quickly she had agreed to an affair with Micah two years ago. She had dated in college and had slept with a couple of the guys. The sex between them hadn't been anything to write home about. She had eventually reached the conclusion that she and sex didn't work well together, which had always been just fine and dandy to her. So when she'd felt the sparks fly between her and Micah in a way she'd never felt before, she'd believed the attraction was something worth exploring.

Kalina nibbled on her bottom lip, thinking that was then, this was now. She had learned her lesson regarding Micah. They shared a chemistry that hadn't faded with time. If he thought she had the cutest dimples then she could say the same about his lips. She could imagine her tongue gliding over them for a taste, and it wouldn't be a quick one.

She shook her head. Her thoughts were really getting out of hand, and it was time to rein them back in. Today had been a busy day, filled with numerous activities and a conference call with Washington that had lasted a couple of hours. More than once, she had glanced up from her notes to find Micah staring at her. And each time their gazes connected, a wild swirl of desire would try overtaking her senses.

"Have you found anything unusual, Kalina?"

Micah's deep, husky voice broke into her thoughts, reminding her he had entered the room. Not that she'd totally forgotten. She lifted her gaze from the microscope and wished she hadn't. He looked yummy enough to eat. Literally.

He had come to stand beside her. Glancing up at him, she saw the intense concentration in his eyes seemed hot, near blazing. It only made her more aware of the deep physical chemistry radiating between them, which she was trying to ignore but finding almost impossible to do.

"I think you need to take a look at this," she said, moving aside so he could look through her microscope.

He moved in place and she studied him for a minute while he sat on the stool, absorbed in analyzing what she'd wanted him to see. Moments later, he glanced back up at her. "Granulated particles?"

"Yes, that's what they appear to be, and barely noticeable. I plan on separating them to see if I can pinpoint what they are. There's a possibility the substance entering the bloodstream wasn't a liquid like we first assumed."

He nodded, agreeing with her assumption. "Let me know what you find out."

"I will." God, she needed her head examined, but she couldn't shift her gaze away from his lips. Those oh-so-cute lips were making deep-seated feelings stir inside her and take center stage. His lips moved, and it was then she realized he had said something.

"Sorry, did you say something?" she asked, trying to regain her common sense, which seemed to have taken a tumble by the wayside.

"Yes, I said I dreamed about you last night."

She stared at him. Where had that come from? How on earth had they shifted from talking about the findings under her microscope to him having a dream about her?

"And in my dream, I touched you all over. I tasted you all over."

Her heart thudded painfully in her chest. His words left her momentarily speechless and breathless. And it didn't help matters that the tone he'd used was deep, husky and as masculine as any male voice could be. Instead of grating on her nerves, it was grating on other parts of her body. Stroking them into a sensual fever.

She drew in a deep breath and said, "I thought you were going to stay in your place, Micah."

He smiled that sexy, rich smile of his, and she felt something hot and achy take her over. Little pangs of sexual desire, and the need she'd tried ignoring for two years, expanded in full force.

"I *am* staying in my place, Kalina. But do you know what place I love most of all?"

Something told her not to ask but she did anyway. "What?"

"Deep inside you."

She wasn't sure how she remained standing. She was on wobbly legs with a heart rate that was higher than normal. She compressed her lips, shoving to the back of her mind all the things she'd like to do to his mouth. "You have no right to say something like that," she said, shaking off his words as if they were some unpleasant memory.

A crooked smile appeared on his face. "I have every right, especially since you've practically spoiled me for any other woman."

Yeah, right. Did he think she didn't remember the woman who'd picked him up yesterday at the CDC?

"And what happened to your decision not to become involved with a woman who didn't trust you?"

He chuckled. "Nothing happened. I merely mentioned to you that I dreamed about you last night. No harm's done. No real involvement there."

She frowned. He was teasing her, and she didn't like it. A man didn't tell a woman he'd dreamed about her without there being a hint of his desire for an involvement. What kind of game was Micah playing?

"Theo has already made plans for dinner. What about you?"

She answered without thinking. "No, I haven't made any plans."

"Good, then have dinner with me."

She stared at him. He was smooth, but not smooth enough. "We agreed not to become involved."

He chuckled. "Eating is not an involvement, Kalina. It's a way to feed the urges of one's body."

She didn't say anything, but she knew too well about bodily urges. Food wasn't what her body was craving.

"Having dinner with me is not a prerequisite for an affair. It's where two friends, past lovers, colleagues… however you want to describe our relationship…sit down and eat. I know this nice café not far from here. It's one I used to frequent when I was here the last time. I'd like to take you there."

Don't go, an inner voice warned. *All it will take is for you to sit across from him at a table and watch him eat.* The man had a way of moving his mouth that was so downright sensual it was a crying shame. It had taken all she had just to get through breakfast this morning.

"I don't think going out to dinner with you is a good idea," she finally said.

"And why not?"

"Mainly because you forgot to add the word *enemy* to the list to describe our relationship. I don't like you."

He simply grinned. "Well, I happen to like you a lot. And I don't consider us enemies. Besides, you're not the injured party here, I am. I'm an innocent man, falsely accused of something he didn't do."

She turned back to the microscope as she spoke. "I see things differently."

"I know you do, so why can't you go out to eat with me since nothing I say or do will change your mind? I merely invited you to dinner because I noticed you worked through lunch. But if you're afraid to be with me then I—"

"I'm not afraid to be with you."

"So you say," he said, turning to leave. Before reaching the door, he shot her a smile over his shoulder. "If you change your mind about dinner, I'll be leaving here around seven and you can meet me downstairs in the lobby."

Kalina watched him leave. She disliked him, so she wasn't sure why her hormones could respond to him the way they did. The depth of desire she felt around him was unreal. And dangerous. It only heightened the tension between them, and the thought that he wanted them to share dinner filled her with a heat she could very well do without.

The best thing for her to do was to stay in and order room service. That was the safest choice. But then, why should she be a coward? She, of all people, knew that Micah did not have a place in her life anymore. So, despite his mild flirtation—and that's what it was whether he admitted to it or not—she would not succumb. Nor would she lock herself in her room because she couldn't control her attraction to him. It was time that she learned to control her response to him. There would be other assignments when they would work together, and she needed to put their past involvement behind her once and for all.

She stood and checked her watch, deciding she would have dinner with Micah after all. But she would make sure that she was the one in control at all times.

Five

At precisely seven o'clock, Micah stepped out of the elevator hoping he hadn't overplayed his hand. When he glanced around the lobby and saw Kalina sitting on one of the sofas, he felt an incredible sense of relief. He had been prepared to dine alone if it had come to that, but he'd more than hoped that she was willing to dine with him.

He walked over to her. From the expression on her face, it was obvious she was apprehensive about them dining together, so he intended to make sure she enjoyed herself—even as he made sure she remembered what they'd once shared. A shiver of desire raced up his spine when she saw him and stood. She was wearing a dress that reminded him of what a nice pair of legs she had. And her curvy physique seemed made for that outfit.

He had gone over his strategy upstairs in case she joined him. He wouldn't make a big deal of her accompanying him. However, he would let her know he appreciated her being there.

He stopped when he reached her. "Kalina. You look nice tonight."

"Thanks. I think we need to get a couple of things straight."

He figured she would say that. "Let's wait until we get to the restaurant. Then you can let go all you want," he replied, taking her arm and placing it in the crux of his.

He felt her initial resistance before she relaxed. "Fine, but we will have that conversation. I don't have a problem joining you for dinner, but I don't want you getting any ideas."

Too late. He had gotten plenty already. He smiled. "You worry too much. There's no need for me to ask if you trust me because I know you don't. But can you cut me a little slack?"

Kalina held his gaze for a moment longer than he thought necessary, before she released an exasperated breath. "Does it matter to you that I don't particularly like you anymore?"

He took her hand in his to lead her out of the villa. "I'm sorry to hear that because I definitely like you. Always have. From the first."

She rolled her eyes. "So you say."

He chuckled. "So I know."

She pulled her hand from his when they stepped outside. The air was cool, and he thought it was a smart thing that she'd brought along a shawl. He could visualize her wrapped up in it and wearing nothing else.

She had done that once, and he could still remember her doing so. It had been a red one with fringes around the hem. He had shown up at the hotel where they were staying in Sydney with their take-out dinner, and she had emerged from the bedroom looking like a lush red morsel. She had ended up being his treat for the night.

"Micah?"

He glanced over when he realized she'd said something. "Yes?"

"Are we walking or taking a cab?"

"We'll take a cab and tell the driver not to hurry so we can enjoy the beautiful view. Unless, however, you prefer to walk. It's not far away, within walking distance."

"Makes no difference to me," she said, moving her gaze from his to glance around.

'In that case, we'll take the cab. I know how much you like a good ride."

Kalina's face flushed after she heard what Micah said. There was no way he could convince her he hadn't meant what she thought he'd meant. That innocent look on his face meant nothing. But then, he, of all people, knew how much she liked to be on top and he'd always accommodated her. She just loved the feel of being on top of a body so well built and fine it could make even an old woman weep in pleasure.

She decided that if he was waiting on a response to his comment, he would be disappointed because she didn't intend to give him one. She would say her piece at the restaurant.

"Here's our cab."

The bellman opened the door for her. Kalina slid in

the back and Micah eased in right behind her. The cab was small but not small enough where they needed to be all but sitting in each other's lap. "You have plenty of space over there," she said, pointing to Micah's side.

Without any argument he slid over, but then he turned and flashed those pearly-white teeth as he smiled at her. Her gaze narrowed. "Any reason you find me amusing?"

He shrugged. "I don't. But I do find you sexy as hell."

That was a compliment she didn't need and opened her mouth to tell him so, then closed it, deciding to leave well enough alone. He would be getting an earful soon enough.

When he continued to sit there and stare at her, she found it annoying and asked, "I thought you said you were going to enjoy the view."

"I am."

God, how had she forgotten how much he considered seduction an art form? Of course, he should know that using that charm on her was a wasted effort. "Can I ask you something, Micah?"

"Baby, you can ask me anything."

She hated to admit that his term of endearment caused a whirling sensation in her stomach. "Why are you doing this? Saying those things? I'm sure you're well aware it's a waste of your time."

"Is it?"

"Yes."

He didn't say anything for a moment and then, "To answer your question, the reason I'm doing this and saying all these things is that I'm hoping you'll remember."

She didn't have to ask what he wanted her to remember. She knew. Things had been good between them. Every night. Every morning. He'd been the best lover a woman could have and she had appreciated those nights spent in his arms. And speaking of those arms...they were hidden in a nice shirt that showed off the wide breadth of his shoulders. She knew those shoulders well and used to hold on to him while she rode him mercilessly. And then there were his hands. Beautiful. Strong. Capable of delivering mindless pleasure. And they were hands that would travel all over her body, touching her in places no man had touched her before and leaving a trail of heat in their wake.

Her gaze traveled upward past his throat to his mouth. It lingered there while recalling the ways he would use that mouth to make her scream. Oh, how she would scream while he took care of that wild, primal craving deep within her.

Gradually, her gaze left his mouth to move upward and stared into the depth of his bedroom-brown eyes. They were staring straight at her, pinning her in place and almost snatching the air from her lungs with their intensity. She wished she could dismiss that stare. Instead she was ensnarled by it in a way that increased her heart rate. An all-too-familiar ache settled right between her thighs. He was making her want something she hadn't had since he'd given it to her.

"Do you remember all the things we used to do behind closed doors, Kalina?"

Yes, she remembered and doubted she could ever forget. Sex between them had been good. The best. But it had all been a lie. That memory of his betrayal cut through her desire and forced a laugh from deep within her throat. "I've got to hand it to you, Micah. You're good."

He shrugged and then said in a low, husky tone, "You always said I was."

Yes, she had and it had been the truth. "Yes, but you're not good enough to get me into bed ever again. If you'll recall, I know the reason you slept with me." She was grateful for the glass partition that kept the cabby from hearing their conversation.

"I know the reason, as well. I wanted you. Pure and simple. From the moment you walked into that ballroom on your father's arm, I knew I wanted you. And being with you in Sydney afforded me the opportunity to have you. I wanted those legs wrapped around me, while I stroked you inside out. I wanted to bury my head between your thighs, to know the taste of you, and I wanted you to know the taste of me."

Her traitorous body began responding to his words. Myriad sensations were rolling around in her stomach. "It was all about sex, then," she said, trying to once again destroy the heated moment.

He nodded. "Yes, in the beginning. That's why I gave you my ground rules. But then…"

She shouldn't ask but couldn't help doing so. "But then what?" she asked breathlessly.

"And then the hunter got captured by the prey."

She opened her mouth and then closed it when the cabdriver told them via a speaker that they'd arrived. She glanced out the window. It was a beautiful restaurant—quaint and romantic.

He opened the door and reached for her hand. The reaction to his touch instantly swept through her. The man could make her ache without even trying.

"You're going to like the food here," he said, helping her out of the cab and not releasing her hand. She wanted to pull it from his grasp, but the feel of that one lone finger stroking her palm kept her hand where it was.

"I'm sure I will."

They walked side by side into the restaurant and she couldn't recall the last time they'd done so. It had felt good, downright giddy, being the center of Micah Westmoreland's attention and he had lavished it on her abundantly.

She didn't know what game Micah was playing tonight or what he was trying to prove. The only thing she did know was that by the time they left this restaurant he would know where she stood, and he would discover that she didn't intend to be a part of his game playing.

"The food here is delicious, Micah."

He smiled. "Thanks. I was hoping you would join me since I knew you would love everything they had on the menu. The last time I was here, this was my favorite place to eat."

He recalled the last time he'd been in Bajadad. He'd felt guilty about being so far away from home, so far away from his family, especially when the younger Westmorelands, who'd taken his parents' and aunt's and uncle's deaths hard, had rebelled like hell. Getting a call from Dillon to let him know their youngest brother, Bane, had gotten into trouble again had become a common occurrence.

"We need to talk, Micah."

He glanced across the table at Kalina and saw the firm set of her jaw. He'd figured she would have a lot to say, so he'd asked that they be given a private room in the back. It was a nice room with a nice view, but nothing was nicer than looking at the woman he was with.

He now knew he had played right into her father's hands just as much as she had. The general had been certain that Micah would be so pissed that Kalina didn't believe him that he wouldn't waste his time trying to convince her of the truth. He hadn't. He had allowed two years to pass while the lie she believed festered.

But now he was back, seeking her forgiveness. Not for what he had done but for what he hadn't done, which was to fight for her and to prove his innocence. Dillon had urged him to do that as soon as Kalina had confronted him, but Micah had been too stubborn, too hurt that she could so easily believe the worst about him. Now he wished he had fought for her.

"Okay, you can talk and I'll listen," he said, pushing his plate aside and taking a sip of his wine.

She frowned and blew out a breath. "I want you to stop with the game playing."

"And that's what you think I'm doing?"

"Yes."

He had news for her, what he was doing was fighting for his survival the only way he knew how. He intended to make her trust him. He would lower his guard and include her in his world, which is something he hadn't done since Patrice. He would seduce her back into a relationship and then prove she was wrong. He would do things differently this time and show her he wasn't the man she believed him to be.

"What if I told you that you're wrong?"

"Then what do you call what you're doing?" she asked in a frustrated tone.

"Pursuing the woman I want," he said simply.

"To get me in your bed?"

"Or any other way I can get you. It's not all sexual."

She gave a ladylike snort. "And you expect me to believe that?"

He chuckled. "No, not really. You've told me numerous times that you don't believe a word I say."

"Then why are you doing this? Why would you want to run behind a woman who doesn't want you?"

"But you *do* want me."

She shook her head. "No, I don't."

He smiled. "Yes, you do. Even though you dislike me for what you think I did, there's a part of you that wants me as much as I want you. Should I prove it?"

She narrowed her gaze. "You can't prove anything."

He preferred to disagree but decided not to argue with her. "All right."

She lifted her brow. "So you agree with what I said?"

"No, but I'm not going to sit here and argue with you about it."

She inclined her head. "We are not arguing about it, we are discussing it. Things can't continue this way."

"So what do you suggest?"

"That you cease the flirtation and sexual innuendoes. I don't need them."

Micah was well acquainted with what she needed. It was the same thing he needed. A night together. But sharing one night would just be a start. Once he got her back in his bed he intended to keep her there. Forever. He drew in a deep breath. The thought of forever with any other woman was enough to send him into a panic. But not with her.

He placed his napkin on the table as he glanced over at her. "Since you've brought them up, let's take a moment to talk about needs, shall we?"

She nodded. That meant she would at least listen, although he knew in the end she wouldn't agree to what he was about to suggest. "Although our relationship two years ago got off on a good start, it ended on a bad note. I'm not going to sit here and rehash all that happened, everything you've falsely accused me of. At first I was pretty pissed off that you would think so low of me. Then I realized the same thing you said a couple of nights ago at that party—you didn't know me. I never gave you the chance to know the real me. If you'd known the real *me* then you would not have believed the lie your father told you."

She didn't say anything, but he knew that didn't necessarily mean she was agreeing with him. In her eyes, he was guilty until proven innocent. "I want you to get to know the real me, Kalina."

She took a sip of her wine and held his gaze. "And how am I supposed to do that?"

At least she had asked. "You and I both have a thirty-day leave coming up as soon as we fly out of India. I'd like to invite you to go home with me."

Kalina sat up straight in her chair. "Go home with you?"

"Yes."

She stared at him across the lit candle in the middle of the table. "And where exactly is home?"

"Denver. Not in the city limits, though. My family and I own land in Colorado."

"Your family?"

"Yes, and I would love for you to meet them. I have fourteen brothers and cousins, total, that live in Denver. And then there are those cousins living in Atlanta, Montana and Texas."

This was the first time he'd mentioned anything about his family to her, except for the day he had briefly spoken of his parents when she'd asked. "What a diverse family." She didn't have any siblings or cousins. He was blessed to have so many.

He leaned back in his chair with his gaze directly on her. "So, will you come?"

"No." She hadn't even needed to think about it. There was no reason for her to spend her vacation time with Micah and his family. What would it accomplish?

As if he had read her mind, he said, "It would help mend things between us."

She narrowed her gaze. "Why would I want them mended?"

"Because you are a fair person, and I believe deep down you want to know the truth as much as I want you to. For whatever reason—and I have my suspicions as to what they are—your father lied about me. I need to redeem myself."

"No, you don't."

"Yes, I do, Kalina. Whether there's ever anything between us again matters to me. Like I told you before, I truly did enjoy the time we spent together, and I think if you put aside that stubborn pride of yours, you'll admit that you did, too."

He was right, she had. But the pain of his betrayal

was something she hadn't been able to get beyond. "What made you decide to invite me to your home, Micah?"

"I told you. I want you to get to know me."

She narrowed her gaze. "Could it be that you're also planning for us to sleep together again?"

His mouth eased into a smile, and he took another sip of his wine. "I won't lie to you. That thought had crossed my mind. But I have never forced myself on any woman and I don't ever plan to do so. I would love to share a bed with you, Kalina, but the purpose of this trip is for you to get to know me. And I also want you to meet my family."

She set down her glass. "Why do you want me to get to know your family now, Micah, when you didn't before?"

Kalina noted the serious expression that descended upon his features. Was she mistaken or had her question hit a raw nerve? Leaning back in her chair, she stared at him while waiting for an answer. Given that he'd invited her to his home to meet his family, she felt she deserved one.

He took another sip of wine and, for a moment, she thought he wasn't going to answer and then he said. "Her name was Patrice Nelson. I met her in my second year of college. I was nineteen at the time. We dated only a short while before I knew she was the one. I assumed she thought the same thing about me. We had been together a few months when a plane carrying my parents went down, killing everyone on board, including my father's brother and his wife."

She gasped, and a sharp pain hit her chest. She had known about his parents, but hadn't known other family members had been killed in that plane crash, as well. "You lost your parents and your aunt and uncle?"

"Yes. My father and his brother were close and so were my mother and my aunt. They did practically everything together, which was the reason they were on the same plane. They had gone away for the weekend. My parents had seven kids and my aunt and uncle had eight. That meant fifteen Westmorelands were left both motherless and fatherless. Nine of them were under the age of sixteen at the time."

"I'm sorry," she said, feeling a lump in her throat. She hadn't known him at the time, but she could still feel his pain. That had to have been an awful time for him.

"We all managed to stay together, though," he said, breaking into her thoughts.

"How?"

"The oldest of all the Westmorelands was my brother Dillon. He was twenty-one and had just graduated from the university and had been set to begin a professional basketball career. He gave it all up to come home. Dillon, and my cousin Ramsey, who was twenty, worked hard to keep us together, even when people were encouraging him to put the younger four in foster homes. He refused. Dil, with Ramsey's help, kept us all together."

In his voice, she could hear the admiration he had for his brother and cousin. She then recalled the woman in his life at the time. "And I'm sure this Patrice was there for you during that time, right?"

"Yes, so it seemed. I took a semester off to help with things at home since I'm the third oldest in the family, although there's only a month separating me from my cousin Zane."

He took a sip of wine and then said, "Patrice came to visit me several times while I was out that semester, and she got to know my family. Everyone liked her... at least everyone but one. My cousin Bailey, who was the youngest of the Westmorelands, was barely seven, and she didn't take a liking to Patrice for reasons we couldn't understand."

He didn't say anything for a moment, as if getting his thoughts together, then he continued, "I returned to school that January, arriving a couple of days earlier than planned. I went straight to Patrice's apartment and…"

Kalina lifted a brow. "And what?"

"And I walked in on her in bed with one of her professors."

Of all the things Kalina had assumed he would say, that definitely wasn't one of them. She stared at him, and he stared back. She could see it, there, plain, right in his features—the strained look that came from remembered pain. He had been hurt deeply by the woman's deception.

"What happened after that?" she asked, curious.

"I left and went to my own apartment, and she followed me there. She told me how sorry she was. She said that she felt she needed to be honest with me, as well as with herself, so she also admitted it hadn't been the first time she'd done it with one of her professors, nor would it be the last. She said she needed her degree, wanted to graduate top of her class and saw nothing wrong with what she was doing. She said that if I loved her I would understand."

Kalina's mouth dropped. *The nerve of the hussy assuming something like that!* "And did you understand?"

"No." He didn't say anything for a moment. "Her actions not only hurt me, but they hurt my family. They had liked her and had become used to her being with me whenever I came home. It probably wouldn't have been so bad if Dillon's and Ramsey's girls hadn't betrayed them around the same time. We didn't set a good example for the others as far as knowing how to pick decent and honest women."

He paused a moment and then said in a low, disappointed voice, "I vowed then never to get involved with a woman to the extent that I'd bring her home to my family. And I've kept that promise…until now."

Kalina took a sip of her drink and held Micah's gaze, not knowing what to say. Why was he breaking his vow now, for her? Did it matter that much to him that she got to know him better than she had in Sydney?

Granted, she realized he was right. Other than being familiar with how well he performed in bed, she didn't know the simplest things about him, like his favorite color, his political affiliation or his religious beliefs. Those things might not be important for a short-term affair, but they were essential for a long-term relationship.

But then they'd never committed to a relationship. They had been merely enjoying each other's company and companionship. She hadn't expected "forever" and frankly hadn't been looking for it, either. But that didn't mean the thought hadn't crossed her mind once or twice during their two-month affair.

And she was very much aware that the reason he wanted her to get to know him now still didn't have anything to do with "forever." He assumed if she got to know him then she would see that she'd been wrong to accuse him of manipulating her for her father.

The lump in her throat thickened. What if she was wrong about him and her father had lied? What if she had begun to mean something to Micah the way he claimed? She frowned, feeling a tension headache coming on when so many what-ifs flooded her brain. Her father had never lied to her before, but there was a first time for everything. Perhaps he hadn't outright lied, but she knew how manipulative he could be where she was concerned.

"You don't have to give me your answer tonight, Kal, but please think about it."

She broke eye contact with him to study her wineglass for a moment, twirling the dark liquid around. Then she lifted her gaze to meet his again and said, "Okay, I will think about it."

A smile touched his lips. "Good. That's all I'm asking." He then checked his watch. "Ready to leave?"

"Yes."

Moments later, as they stood outside while a cab was hailed for them, she couldn't help remembering everything Micah had told her. She couldn't imagine any woman being unfaithful to him, and she could tell from the sound of his voice while he'd relayed the story that the pain had gone deep. That had been well over ten years ago. Was he one of those men, like her father, who could and would love only one woman?

She was aware of how her mother's death had affected her father. Although she'd known him to have lady friends over the years, she also knew he hadn't gotten serious about any of them. Her mother, he said, would always have his heart. Kalina couldn't help wondering if this Patrice character still claimed Micah's heart.

When they were settled in the cab, she glanced over at him and said, "I'm sorry."

He lifted a brow. "For what?"

"Your loss. Your parents. Your uncle and aunt." She wouldn't apologize for Patrice because she didn't see her being out of the picture as a loss. Whether he realized it or not, finding out how deceitful his girlfriend was had been a blessing.

His gaze held hers intensely, unflinchingly, when he said, "I didn't share my history with you for your pity or sympathy."

She nodded. "I know." And she did know. He had taken the first steps in allowing her to get beyond that guard he'd put up. For some reason, she felt that he truly wanted her to get to know him. The real Micah Westmoreland. Was he truly any different from the one she already knew?

She had to decide just how much of him, if any, she wanted to get to know. He had invited her to spend time with him and his family in Denver, and she had to think hard if that was something she really wanted to do.

A few hours later, back in his room at the villa, Micah turned off the lamp beside his bed and stared up at the ceiling in darkness. He had enjoyed sharing dinner with Kalina, and doing so had brought back memories of the time they'd spent together in Sydney. Tonight, more than ever, he had been aware of her as a woman. A woman he wanted. A woman he desired. A woman he intended to have.

He'd never wanted to be attracted to Kalina, even in the beginning. Mainly because he'd known she would hold his interest too much and for way too long. But there hadn't been any hope for him. The chemistry had been too strong. The desire too thick. He had been attracted to her in a way he had never been attracted to another woman.

And tonight she had been a good listener. She had asked the questions he had expected her to ask and hadn't asked ones that were irrelevant. The private room they'd been given had been perfect for such a conversation. But even the intense subject matter did nothing to lessen the heat that stirred in the air, or waylay the desire that simmered between them.

Very few people knew the real reason he and Patrice had ended things. He'd only told Dillon, Ramsey and Zane, the cousin he was closest to. Micah was certain the others probably assumed they knew the reason, but he knew their assumptions wouldn't even come close.

Walking in and finding the woman he loved in bed with another man had been traumatic for him, especially given that he'd been going through a very distressing time in his life already. The sad thing was that there hadn't been any remorse because Patrice had felt justified in doing what she'd done. She just hadn't been able to comprehend that normal men and women didn't share their partners.

He shifted in bed and thought about Kalina. He had enjoyed her company tonight and believed she'd enjoyed his. He'd even felt an emotional connection to her, something he hadn't felt with a woman in years. He didn't need to close his eyes to remember the stricken look on her face two years ago when she'd overheard words that had implicated him. And no matter how much he had proclaimed his innocence, she hadn't believed him.

For two years, they had gone their separate ways. At first, he'd been so angry he hadn't given a damn. But at night he would lie in bed awake. Wanting her and missing her. It was then that he'd realized just how much Kalina had worked her way into his bloodstream, how deeply she'd become embedded under his skin. He had traveled to several countries over the past two years. He had worked a ton of hours. But nothing had been able to eradicate Kalina from his mind.

Now she was back in his life, and he intended to use this opportunity to right a wrong. If only she would agree to go home to Denver with him. He wouldn't question why it was so important to him for her to do so, but it was. And although he hadn't told her, he wouldn't accept no for an answer.

So what are you going to do if she turns you down, Westmoreland? Kidnap her?

Kidnapping Kalina didn't sound like a bad idea, but he knew he wouldn't operate on the wrong side of the law. He hoped that she gave his invitation some serious consideration so it didn't come to that.

It had been hard being so close to her and having to keep his hands to himself when he'd wanted them all over her, touching her in places he'd been privy to before. But as he'd told her, it was important that they get to know each other, something they hadn't taken the time to do in Sydney.

On the cab ride back, he'd even discovered she knew how to ride a horse and that her grandparents had been farmers in Alabama. Her grandparents had even raised, among other things, sheep. His cousin Ramsey, who was the sheep rancher in the Westmoreland family, would appreciate knowing that. And Micah couldn't wait to show Kalina his ranch. He hoped she liked it as much as he did. And...

He drew in a deep breath, forcing himself to slow down and put a lid on his excitement. He had to face the possibility that she would decide not to go to Denver. He refused to let that happen. The woman had no idea just how much he wanted her and he intended to do whatever he had to to have her.

If he had to turn up the heat to start breaking down her defenses then that's what he would do.

Six

The next day, Kalina's body tensed when she entered the lab and immediately remembered that she and Micah would be working alone together today. Theo was in another area analyzing the granules taken from the bodies of the five victims.

She eased the door closed behind her and stood leaning against it while she looked over at Micah. He was standing with his head tilted back as he studied the solution in the flask he was holding up to the light. She figured he wasn't aware she had entered, which was just as well for the time being.

His request from last night was still on her mind, and even after a good night's sleep, she hadn't made a decision about what she would do. She had weighed the pros and cons of accompanying him to Denver, but even that hadn't helped. It had been late when she had returned from dinner, but she'd tried reaching her father. The person she'd talked to at the Pentagon wouldn't even tell her his whereabouts, saying that, at the moment, the general's location was confidential. She had wanted to hear her father tell her again how Micah had played a role in keeping her out of China. A part of her resented the fact that Micah was back in her life, but another part of her felt she deserved to know the truth.

She wrapped her arms around herself, feeling a slight damp in the air. Everyone had awakened to find it raining that morning. And although the showers only lasted for all of ten minutes, it had been enough to drench the mountainside pretty darn good.

Micah's back was to her, and her gaze lowered to his backside, thinking it was one part of his body she'd always admired. He certainly had a nice-looking butt. She'd heard from Theo that Micah had gotten up before five this morning to go to the villa's gym to work out. She would have loved to have been a fly on the wall, to watch him flex those masculine biceps of his.

Her thoughts drifted to the night before. On the cab ride back to the villa he'd told her more about his brothers and cousins. She wasn't sure if he was feeding her curiosity or deliberately enticing her to want to meet them all for herself. And she would admit that she'd become intrigued. But was that enough to make her want to spend an entire month with him in Denver?

"Are you going to just stand there or get to work? There's plenty of it to be done."

She frowned, wondering if he had eyes in the back of his head, as he'd yet to turn around. "How did you know it was me?"

"Your scent gave you away, like it always does."

Since she usually wore the same cologne every day, she would let that one slide. She moved away from the door at the same time as he turned around, and she really wished he hadn't when he latched those dark, intense eyes onto her. Evidently, this was going to be one of her "drool over Micah" days. She'd had a number of them before. He was looking extremely handsome today. He probably looked the same yesterday, but today her hormones were out in full force, reminding her just how much of a woman she was and reminding her of all those sexual needs she had ignored for two years.

"Have most of the tissues been analyzed?" she asked, sliding onto her stool in front of a table that contained skin samples taken during autopsies of the five victims.

"No, I left that for you to do."

"No problem."

She glanced over at Micah, who was still studying the flask while jotting down notes. He was definitely engrossed in his work. Last night, he'd been engrossed in her. Was this the same man whose gaze had filled her with heated lust last night during the cab rides to the restaurant and back? The same man who'd sat across from her at dinner with a look that said he wanted to eat her alive? The same man whose flirtation and sexual innuendoes had stirred her with X-rated sensations? The same man who exuded a virility that said he was all man, totally and completely?

"Are you going to get some work done or sit there and waste time daydreaming?"

She scowled, not appreciating his comment. Evidently, he wasn't in a good mood. She wondered who had stolen his favorite toy. Now he was sitting on a stool at the counter and hadn't glanced up.

"For your information, I get paid for the work I do and not the time it takes me to do it."

She shook her head. And to think that this was the same man who'd wanted her to spend thirty days with him and his family. She'd have thought he would be going out of his way to be nice to her.

"In other words…"

"In other words, Dr. Westmoreland," she said, placing her palms on the table and leaning forward. "I can handle my business."

He looked up at her and his mouth twitched in a grin. "Yes, Dr. Daniels, I know for a fact that you most certainly can."

She narrowed her eyes when it became obvious he'd been doing nothing more than teasing her. "I was beginning to wonder about you, Micah."

"In what respect?" he asked.

"Your sanity."

"Ouch."

"Hey, you had that coming," she said, and couldn't help the smile that touched her lips.

"I wish I had something else coming about now. My sanity as well as my body could definitely use it."

Her eyebrows lifted. The look in his eyes, the heated lust she saw in their dark depths told her they were discussing something that had no place in the lab. Deciding it was time to change the subject, she said, "How are things going? Found anything unusual?"

He shook his head. "Other than what you found yesterday, no, I could find nothing else. Theo's dissecting those tissue particles now. Maybe he'll come across something else in the breakdown."

She blew out a breath, feeling a degree of frustration. Granted, it was just the second day, but still, she was anxious about those samples Theo was analyzing. So far there hadn't been any more deaths and that was a good thing. But, at the same time, if they couldn't discover the cause, there was a chance the same type of deaths could occur again.

She glanced over at Micah at the exact moment that he raised his head from his microscope. "Come and take a look at this."

There was something in his voice that made her curious. Without thinking, she quickly moved across the room. When he slid off his stool, she slid onto it. She looked down into his microscope and frowned. She then looked up at him, confused. "I don't see anything."

"Then maybe you aren't looking in the right place."

Kalina wasn't sure exactly what she was expecting, but it wasn't Micah reaching out and gently pulling her from the stool to wrap his arms around her. His manly scent consumed her and his touch sent fire racing all through her body. She drew in a steadying breath and tilted her head back to look up at him. And when he brought her closer to his hard frame, she felt every inch of him against her.

Although her pulse was drumming erratically in response, she said, "I don't want this, Micah." She knew it was a lie the moment she said it and, from the heat of his gaze, he knew it was a lie, as well.

"Then maybe I need to convince you otherwise," he said, seconds before lowering his mouth to hers.

She had intended to shove him away...honestly she

had, but the moment she parted her lips on an enraged sigh and he took the opportunity to slide his tongue in her mouth, she was a goner. Her stomach muscles quivered at the intensity and strength in the tongue that caught hold of hers and began sucking as if it had every right to do so. Sucking on her tongue as if it was the last female tongue on earth.

He was devouring her. Feasting on her. Driving her insane while tasting her with a sexual hunger she felt all the way to her toes. A strong concentration of that hunger settled in the juncture of her thighs.

And speaking of that spot, she felt his erection—right there—hard, rigid, pressing against her belly, making her remember a time when it had done more than nudge her, making her remember a time when it had actually slid inside her, between her legs, going all the way to the hilt, touching her womb. It had once triggered her inner muscles to give a possessive little squeeze, just seconds before they began milking his aroused body for everything they could get and forcing him to explode in an out-of-this-world orgasm. She remembered. She couldn't forget.

And then she began doing something she was driven to do because of the way he was making love to her mouth, as well as the memories overtaking her. Just like the last time he'd overstepped his boundaries in a kiss, she began kissing him back, taking the lead by escaping the captivity of his tongue and then capturing his tongue with hers. Ignoring the conflicting emotions swamping her, she kissed him in earnest, with a hunger only he could stir. She took possession of his mouth and he let her. He was allowing her to do whatever she wanted. Whatever pleased her. And when she heard a deep guttural moan, she wasn't sure if it had come from his throat or hers.

At the moment she really didn't care.

Micah deepened the kiss, deciding it was time for him to take over. Or else he would have Kalina stretched across the nearest table with her legs spread so fast neither of them would have a chance to think about the consequences. He doubted he would ever get tired of kissing her and was surprised this was just the second time their tongues had mingled since seeing each other again. But then, staying away from each other had been her decision, not his. If he had his way, their mouths would be locked together 24/7.

As usual, she fit perfectly in his arms, and she felt as if she belonged there. There was nothing like kissing a beautiful woman, especially one who could fill a man's head with steamy dreams at night and heated reality during the day. He found it simply amazing, the power a woman could wield over a man. Case in point, the power that this particular woman had over him.

It didn't matter when he kissed her, or how often, he always wanted more of her. There was nothing quite like having her mouth beneath his. And he liked playing the tongue game with her. He would insert his tongue into her mouth and deepen the kiss before withdrawing and then going back in. He could tell from her moans that she was enjoying the game as much as he was.

His aroused body was straining hard against his zipper, begging for release, pleading for that part of her it had gotten to know so well in Australia. Her feminine scent was in the air, feeding his mind and body with a heated lust that had blood rushing through his body.

A door slamming somewhere had them quickly pulling apart, and he watched as she licked her lips as if she could still taste him there. His guts clenched at the thought. He'd concluded from the first that she had a very sexy mouth, and from their initial kiss he'd discovered that not only was it sexy, it was damn tasty as sin. She took a step back and crossed her arms over her chest, pulling in quick breaths. "I can't believe you did that. What if someone had walked in on us?"

He shrugged while trying to catch his own breath. His mouth was filled with her taste, yet he wanted more. "Then I would have been pretty upset about the interruption," he said.

She glared. "We should be working."

He smiled smoothly. "We are. However, we are entitled to breaks." He leaned against the table. "I think you need to loosen up a little."

"And I think you need to get a grip. You've gotten your kiss, Micah. That's two now. If I were you, I wouldn't try for a third."

He had news for her, he would try for a third, fourth, fifth and plenty more beyond that. There was no way his mouth wouldn't be locking with hers again. She had sat back down on the stool and had picked up one of the vials as if to dismiss not only him but also what they'd just shared. He had no intention of letting her do that. "Why can't we kiss again? I'm sure there's plenty more where those two came from."

She lifted her gaze to his. "I beg to differ."

He chuckled. "Oh, I plan to have you begging, all right."

Her eyes narrowed, and he thought she looked absolutely adorable. Hot, saucy and totally delectable. "If you're trying to impress me then—"

"I'm not. I want you to get to know me and the one thing you'll discover about me is that I love the unexpected. I like being unpredictable, and when it comes to you, I happen to be addicted."

"Thanks for letting me know. I will take all that into consideration while deciding if I'm going home with you in a couple of weeks. You might as well know none of it works in your favor."

"I never took you for a coward."

She frowned. "Being a coward has nothing to do with it. It's using logical thinking and not giving in to whims. Maybe you should do the same."

He couldn't help the grin that spread across his lips. Lips that still carried her taste. "Oh, sweetheart, I *am* using logical thinking. If I got any more sensible I would have stripped you naked by now instead of just imagining doing it. In fact, I'm doing more than imagining it, I'm anticipating it happening. And when it does, I promise to make it worth every moan I get out of you."

Ignoring her full-fledged glare, he glanced at his watch. "I think I'll go grab some lunch. I've finished logging my findings on today's report, but if you need help with what you have to do then—"

"Thanks for the offer, but I can handle things myself."

"No problem. And just so we have a clear understanding… My invitation to go home with me to Denver has no bearing on my kissing you, touching you or wanting to make love to you. You have the last word."

She raised an eyebrow. "Do I really?"

"Absolutely. But I'd like to warn you not to say one thing while your body says another. I tend to listen more to body language."

"Thanks for the warning."

"And thanks for the kiss," he countered.

She frowned, and he smiled. If only she knew what he had in store for her... Hell, it was a good thing that she didn't know. His smile widened as he removed his lab jacket. "I'll be back later. Don't work too hard while I'm gone. You might want to start storing up your energy."

"Storing up my energy for what?"

He leaned in close, reached out, lightly stroked her cheek with his fingertips and whispered, "For when we make love again."

Seeing the immediate flash of fire in her gaze, he said, "Not that I plan on gloating, but when you find out the truth, that I've been falsely accused, I figure you'll want to be nice to me. And when you do, I'll be ready. I want you to be ready, as well. I can't wait to make love to you again, and I plan to make it worth the hell you've put me through, baby."

The heat in her gaze flared so hotly he had to struggle not to pull her back into his arms and go after that third kiss. He was definitely going to enjoy pushing her buttons.

As he moved to walk out of the lab, he thought that if that last kiss was anything to go by, he might as well start storing up some energy, as well. He turned back around before opening the door and his gaze traveled over her. He wanted her to feel the heat, feel his desire. He wanted her to want to make love to him as much as he wanted to make love to her.

She held his gaze with a defiant frown and said nothing. He smiled and gave her a wink before finally opening the door to leave.

"It's all his fault," Kalina muttered angrily as she tossed back her covers to ease out of bed. It had been almost a week since that kiss in the lab and she hadn't had a single good night's sleep since.

She was convinced he was deliberately trying to drive her loony. Although he hadn't taken any more liberties with her, he had his unique ways of making her privy to his lusty thoughts. His eye contact told her everything—regardless of whether it was his lazy perusal or his intense gaze—whenever she looked into his eyes there was no doubt about what was on his mind. More than once she'd looked up from her microscope to find those penetrating dark eyes trained directly on her.

It didn't take much to get her juices flowing, literally, and for the past week he'd been doing a pretty good job of it. She knew he enjoyed getting on her last nerve, and it seemed that particular nerve was a hot wire located right at the juncture of her thighs.

She had tried pouring her full concentration into her work. All the test results on the tissues had come back negative. Although they suspected that some deadly virus had killed those five people, as of yet the team hadn't been able to pinpoint a cause, or come up with conclusive data to support their hypothesis. The granules were still a mystery, and so far they had not been able to trace the source. The Indian government was determined not to make a big to-do about what they considered nothing and wouldn't let them test any others who'd gotten sick but had recovered. The team had reported their findings to Washington. The only thing left was to wrap things up. She knew that Micah was still concerned and had expressed as much in his report. A contagious virus was bad enough, but one that could not be traced was even worse.

Although it had been over a week since he'd issued his invitation, she still hadn't given Micah an answer regarding going with him to Denver. With only three days before they left India, he had to be wondering about her decision. Unfortunately, she still didn't have a clue how she would answer him. The smart thing would be to head for Florida for a month, especially since Micah hadn't made the past week easy for her. He deliberately tested her sanity every chance he got. And although he hadn't tried kissing her again, more than once he had intentionally gotten close to her, brushed against her for no reason at all or set up a situation where he was alone with her. Those were the times he would do nothing but stare at her with a heated gaze as potent as any caress.

Kalina drew in a deep breath, suddenly feeling hot and in need of cool air. After slipping into her robe, she crossed the room and pushed open the French doors to step out on the balcony. She appreciated the whisper of a breeze that swept across her face. The chill made her shiver but still didn't put out the fire raging inside her.

Over the past two years she'd gone each day without caring that she was denying her body's sexual needs. Now, being around Micah was reminding her of just what she'd gone without. Whenever she was around him, she was reminded of how it felt to have fingertips stroke her skin, hands touch her all over and arms pull her close to the warmth of a male body.

She missed the caress of a man's lips against hers, the graze of a male's knuckles across her breasts, the lick of a man's tongue and the soft stroke of masculine fingers between her legs.

There was nothing like the feel of a man's aroused body sliding inside, distended and engorged, ready to take her on one remarkable ride. Making her pleasure his own. And giving all of himself while she gave everything back to him.

Her breathing quickened and her pulse rate increased at what she could now admit she'd been missing. What she had given up. No other man had brought her abstinence more to the forefront of her thoughts than Micah. She felt hot, deliriously needy, and she stood there a moment in silence, fighting to get her bearings and control the turbulent, edgy desire thrumming through her.

Nothing like this had ever happened to her before. All it took was for her to close her eyes to recall how it felt for Micah's hands to glide over the curve of her backside, cup it in his large palms and bring her closer to his body and his throbbing erection.

The memories were scorching, hypnotic and almost more than she could handle. But she would handle them. She had no choice. She would not let Micah get the best of her. She had no qualms, however, about getting the best of him—in the area right below his belt.

She rubbed her hand down her face, not believing her thoughts. They had gotten downright racy lately, and she blamed Micah for it. She was just about to turn to go back inside when a movement below her balcony caught her attention. A man was out jogging and she couldn't help noticing what a fine specimen of a man he was.

The temperature outside had to be in the low thirties, yet he was wearing a T-shirt and a pair of shorts. In her opinion, he was pneumonia just waiting to happen. Who in their right mind would be out jogging at this hour of the night, half dressed?

She leaned against the railing and squinted her eyes in the moonlight. That's when she saw that the man who'd captured her attention was Micah. Evidently, she wasn't the only one who couldn't sleep. She found that interesting and couldn't help wondering if perhaps the same desire that was keeping her awake had him in its lusty clutches, as well.

Serves him right if it did. He had spent a lot of his time this week trying his best to tempt her into his bed, but apparently he was getting the backlash.

He was about to jog beneath her balcony, so she held her breath to keep him from detecting her presence. Except for the glow of the half moon, it was dark, and there was no reason for him to glance up…or so she reasoned. But it didn't stop him from doing so. In fact, as if he'd sensed she was there, he slowed to a stop and stared straight up at her, locking in on her gaze.

And he kept right on staring at her while her heart rate increased tenfold. Suddenly there was more than a breeze stirring the air around her, and it seemed as if her surroundings got extremely quiet. The only thing that was coming in clear was the sound of her irregular breathing.

She stared right back at him and saw that his gaze was devouring her in a way she felt clear beneath her robe. In fact, if she didn't know for certain she was wearing clothes, she would think that she was naked. Oh, why were the sensual lines of his lips so well-defined in the moonlight? Knowing she could be headed for serious trouble if their gazes continued to connect, she broke eye contact, only to be drawn back to his gaze seconds later.

He had to be cold, she thought, yet he was standing in that one spot, beneath her balcony, staring up at her. She licked her lips and felt his gaze shift to her mouth.

Then he spoke in a deep, husky voice, "Meet me in the staircase, Kalina."

His request flowed through her, touching her already aroused body in places it shouldn't have. Turbulent emotions swept through her, and from the look in his eyes it was obvious that he expected her to act on his demand. Should she? Could she? Why would she?

She was bright enough to know that he didn't want her to meet him so they could discuss the weather. Nor would they discuss their inability to pinpoint the origin of the deadly virus. There was no doubt in her mind as to why he wanted to meet her on the stairs, and she would be crazy, completely insane, to do what he asked.

Breaking eye contact with him, she moved away from the balcony's railing and slid open the French doors to go back inside. She moved toward her bed, tossed off her robe and was about to slide between the sheets, when she paused. Okay, she didn't like him anymore, but why was she denying herself a chance to have a good night's sleep? She had needs that hadn't been met in more than two years, and she knew for a fact that he was good at that sort of thing. She didn't love him, and he didn't love her. It would be all about needs and wants being satisfied, nothing more.

She drew in a deep breath, thinking she might be jumping the gun here. All he'd asked her to do was to meet him at the stairs. For all she knew, he might just want to talk. Or maybe he merely wanted to kiss her. She gave herself a mental shake, knowing a kiss would only be the start. Any man who looked at her the way Micah had looked at her a few moments ago had more than kissing on his mind.

Deciding to take the guesswork out of it, she reached for the blouse and skirt she'd taken off earlier and quickly put them on. She knew what she wanted, and Micah better not be playing games with her, because she wasn't in the mood.

Heaven help her, but she was only in the mood for one thing, and at the moment, she didn't care whether she liked him or not just as long as he eased that ache within her.

As she grabbed her room key off the nightstand and shoved it into the pocket of her skirt, she headed toward the door.

Micah paced the stairway, trying to be optimistic. Kalina would come. Although he knew it would be a long shot if she did, he refused to give up hope. He had read that look in her eyes. It had been the same one he knew was in his. She wanted him as much as he wanted her. He had been playing cat-and-mouse games with her all week, to the point where Theo had finally pulled him aside and told him to do something about his attitude problem. He'd almost laughed in his friend's face.

Nothing was wrong with his attitude; it was his body that had issues.

So here he was. Waiting. Hoping she wouldn't walk through the door just to tell him to go to hell. Well, he would have news for her. As far as he was concerned, he was already there. Going without a woman for two years hadn't been a picnic, but he hadn't wanted anyone except her and had denied himself because of it. It was unbelievable how a man's desire for one woman could rule his life, dictate his urges and serve as a thermostat for his constant craving. He was feeling the heat. It was flooding his insides and taking control of every part of his being.

Over the past several days, he'd thought about knocking on Kalina's door but had always talked himself out of it. He wouldn't have been so bold as to ask her to meet him on the staircase tonight if he hadn't seen that particular look in her eyes. He knew that look in a woman's eyes well enough: heated lust. He'd seen it in Kalina's eyes many times.

He turned when he heard footsteps. It was late. Most normal people were asleep. He should be asleep. Instead, he was up, wide awake, horny as hell and lusting after a woman. But not just any woman. He wanted Kalina. She still hadn't told him whether she'd made a decision about going home with him, and he hoped that no news was good news.

He heard the sound of the knob turning and his gaze stayed glued to the door. Most people used the elevator. He preferred the stairs when jogging, for the additional workout. He drew in a deep breath. Was it her? Had she really come after two years of separation and the misunderstanding that still existed between them?

The door slowly opened, and he gradually released his breath. It was Kalina, and at that moment, as his gaze held tight to hers, he couldn't stop looking at her. The more he looked at her, the more he wanted her. The more he needed to be with her.

Had to be with her.

But he needed her to want to be with him just as much. Deciding not to take her appearance here for granted, he slowly moved toward her, his steps unhurried yet precise. His breathing was coming out just as hard as the erection he felt pressing against his shorts.

Micah reached her and lifted his hand to push a lock of hair from her face. Knowing what she thought was the truth about him, he understood that it had taken a lot for her to come to him. He intended to make sure she didn't regret it.

He opened his mouth to say something, but she placed a finger to his lips. "Please don't say anything, Micah. Just do it. Take me now and take me hard."

Her words fired his blood, and his immediate thought was that, given the degree of his need, he would have no problem doing that. He tightened his hand on hers. "Come on, let's go up to my room."

She pulled back and shook her head. "No. Do it here. Now."

He met her gaze, stared deep into her eyes. "I wouldn't suggest that if I were you," he warned. "You just might get what you ask for."

"I'm hoping."

He heard the quiver in her voice and saw the degree of urgency in her expression. There was a momentous need within her that was hitting him right in the gut and stirring his own need. He drew in a deep breath.

There was no doubt in his mind that he was about to lose focus, but he also knew he was about to gain something more rewarding.

He then thought of something. *Damn, damn and triple damn.* "I don't have a condom on me."

His words didn't seem to faze her. She merely nodded and said, "I'm still on the pill and still in good health."

"I'm still in good health, as well," he said and thought there was no need to admit that he hadn't made love to another woman since her.

"Then do it, Micah."

He heard the urgency and need in her voice. "Whatever you want, baby."

Reaching behind her, he locked the entry door before lifting her off her feet to place her back against the wall. Raising her skirt, he spread her legs so they could wrap around him. His shaft began twitching, hardening even more as he lowered his zipper to release it. He skimmed his hands between Kalina's legs and smiled when he saw there were no panties he needed to dispense with. She was hot, and ready.

So was he.

He lowered his head to take her mouth, and at the same moment he aimed his erection straight for her center and began sliding in. Her hands on his shoulders were used to draw him closer into the fit of her.

She took in several deep breaths as he became more entrenched in her body. She felt tight, and her inner muscles clenched him. He broke off the kiss, closed his eyes and threw his head back as he clutched her hips and bottom in his hands and went deeper and deeper. There was nothing like having your manhood gripped, pulled and squeezed by feminine muscles intent on milking you dry.

His lips returned to hers in a deep, openmouthed kiss as he began thrusting hard inside her, tilting her body so he could hit her G-spot. He wanted to drive her wild, over the edge.

"Micah. Oh, Micah, don't stop. Please don't stop. I missed this."

She wasn't alone. He had missed this, as well. At that moment, something fierce and overpowering tore through him and like a jackhammer out of control, he thrust inside her hard, quick and deep. Being inside her this way was driving him over the edge, sending fire through his veins and rushing blood to all parts of his body, especially the part connected to her.

"Micah!"

Her orgasm triggered his as hard and hot desire raged through him. He plunged deeper into her body. The explosion mingled their juices as his release shot straight to her womb as if that's where it wanted to be, where it belonged. She shuddered uncontrollably, going over the edge. He followed her there.

Unable to resist, he used his free hand to push aside her blouse and bra and then latched his mouth to her nipple, sucking hard. At the same time, his body erupted into yet another orgasm and a second explosion rocketed him to heights he hadn't scaled in two years.

He now knew without a doubt what had been missing in his life. Kalina. Now more than ever he intended to make sure she never left him again.

Seven

Kalina slowly opened her eyes. Immediately, she knew that although she was in her room at the villa, she was not in bed alone. Her backside was spooned against hard masculine muscles with an engorged erection against the center of her back.

She drew in a deep breath as memories of the night before consumed her. Micah had a way of making her feel feminine and womanly each and every time he kissed her, touched her or made love to her. And he had made love to her several times during the night. It was as if they were both trying to make up for the two years they'd been apart.

Considering the unfinished business between them, she wasn't sure their insatiable passion had been a good thing. But last night she hadn't cared. Her needs had overridden her common sense. Instead of concentrating on what he had done to betray her, she had been focused on what he could do to her body. What he had done last night had taken the edge off, and she had needed it as much as she'd needed to breathe. He had gone above and beyond the call of duty and had satisfied her more than she had imagined possible. Now all she wanted to do was stay in bed, be lazy and luxuriate in the afterglow.

"Hey, babe. You awake?" Micah asked while sliding a bare leg over her naked body.

If she hadn't been awake, she was now, she thought when the feel of his erection on her back stiffened even more. She drew in a deep breath, not sure she was ready to converse with him yet. With the sensation of him pressing against her, however, she had a feeling conversation was the last thing on Micah's mind.

"Kal?"

Knowing she had to answer him sometime, she slowly turned onto her back. "Yes, I'm awake."

He lifted up on his elbow to loom over her and smiled. "Good morning."

She opened her mouth to give him the same greeting, but that was as far as she got. He slid a hand up her hip just seconds before his lips swooped down and captured hers. The second his tongue entered her mouth she was a pathetic goner. No man kissed like Micah. He put everything he was into the kiss, and she could feel all kinds of sensations overtaking her and wrapping her in a sensual cocoon.

A part of her felt that maybe she should pull back. She didn't want to give him the wrong message, but another part of her was in a quandary as to what the wrong message could be, in light of what they'd shared the night before.

And as he kissed her, she remembered every moment of what they'd shared.

She recalled them making love on the stairwell twice before he'd carried her back to her room. Once inside, they had stripped off their clothes and showered together. They'd made out beneath the heated spray of water before lathering each other clean. He had dried her off, only to lick her all over and make her wet again.

Then they had made love in her bed several times. She had ridden him, and he had ridden her. Then they had ridden each other. The last thing she remembered was falling asleep totally exhausted in his arms.

It was Micah who finally pulled his mouth away, but not before using his tongue to lick her lips from corner to corner.

"You need to stop that," she said in a voice that lacked any real conviction.

"I will, when I'm finished with you," he said, nibbling at the corners of her mouth.

She knew that could very well be never. "You need to go to your room so I can get dressed for work, and you need to get dressed, too."

"Later."

And then he was kissing her again, more passionately than before. She tried to ignore the pleasure overtaking her, but she couldn't. So she became a willing recipient and took everything he was giving her. His kiss was so strong and potent that when he finally pulled his mouth away, she actually felt light-headed.

"I missed that," he murmured, close to her ear. "And I missed this, as well." He moved to slide his body over hers, lifted her hips and entered her in one smooth thrust.

He looked down at her and held her gaze in a breathless moment before moving his body in and out of her. "Being inside you feels so incredibly good, Kal," he whispered, and she thought a woman could get spoiled by this. She certainly had been spoiled during their time in Sydney. So much so that she had suffered through withdrawal for months afterward.

"Oh, baby, you're killing me," Micah growled out, increasing the intensity of his strokes. Kalina begged to differ. He was the one killing her. Her body was the one getting the workout of a lifetime. Blood was rushing through all parts of her, sending shock waves that escalated and touched her everywhere. Never had she been made love to so completely.

All further thought was forced from her mind when he hollered her name just seconds before his body bucked in a powerful orgasm. She felt the essence of his release shoot straight to her womb. The feel of it triggered a riot of sensations, which burst loose within her.

"Micah!"

"I'm here, baby. Let it go. Give yourself to me completely. Don't hold anything back."

She heard his words and tried closing her mind to them but found that she couldn't. She couldn't hold anything back, even if she tried. The strength of her need for him stunned her, but whether she wanted to admit it or not, she knew that what she and Micah were sharing was special. She wanted to believe it was meant just for them.

He continued to hold her, even when he eventually

shifted his body off hers. He'd gotten quiet, and she wondered what he was thinking. As if he'd read her thoughts, he reached out and cupped her chin in his hand then tilted her head so she could look at him and he could look at her.

She felt the heat of his gaze in every part of her body. He brushed a kiss across her lips. "Have dinner with me tonight."

She quickly recalled that dinner after a night of passion was how their last affair had begun. They had slept together one night after work and the next evening he'd taken her out to eat. After dinner, they'd gone back to her place and had been intimately involved for two glorious months.

"We've done that already, Micah."

At his confused look, she added. "Dinner and all that goes with it. Remember Sydney? Different place. Same technique."

He frowned. "Are you trying to say I'm boring you?"

She couldn't help smiling. "Do I look bored? Have I acted bored?"

He laughed. "No to both."

"All right, then. All I meant was that I recall a casual dinner was how things started between us the last time."

"You have to eat."

"Yes, but you don't have to be the one who's always there to feed me. I'm a big girl. I can take care of myself."

"Okay, then," he said, leaning in close to run the tip of his tongue around her earlobe. "What do you want from me?"

She chuckled. "What I got last night and this morning was pretty darn good. I have no complaints."

He lifted his head and frowned down at her. "Shouldn't you want more?"

"Are you prepared to give me more?" she countered.

He seemed to sober with her question. He held her gaze a moment then said, "I want you to get to know the real me, Kal. You never did decide if you're willing to go home with me or not."

Mainly because she'd tried putting the invitation out of her mind. She hadn't wanted to talk about it or even think about it. "I need more time."

"You have only two days left," he reminded her.

Yes, she knew. And she wasn't any closer to making a decision than she had been a week ago. Sleeping together had only complicated things. But she had no regrets. She had needed a sexual release.

She had needed him.

"Well, that's it," Micah told Kalina and Theo several hours later, at the end of the workday. "There haven't been any more reported deaths, and with the case of the few survivors, the Indian government won't let us get close enough to do an examination since we have no proof it's linked and the people did survive."

"The initial symptoms were the same. They could have survived for a number of reasons," Kalina said in frustration.

The only way to assure the U.S. military had a preventative mechanism in place if the virus popped up again was to come up with a vaccine. Micah and his team hadn't been able to do that. The chemicals that had been used were not traceable in the human body after death. And the only sign of abnormality they'd been able to find was the enlargement of the tongue. Other than that, all they had was an unexplained virus that presented as death by natural causes.

She, Theo and Micah knew there was nothing natural about it, but there was nothing they could do in this instance except report their findings to Washington and hope this type of "mysterious illness" didn't pop up again. Before the Indian government had pulled the plug on any further examinations of the survivors, Kalina had managed to obtain blood samples, which she had shipped off to Washington for further study.

"I'm flying out tonight," Theo said, standing. "I'm meeting Renee in Paris for one of her shows. Where are you two headed now?"

"I'm headed home to Denver," Micah said. He then glanced over at Kalina expectantly.

Without looking at Micah, she said. "I'm not sure where I'm going yet."

"Well, you two take care of yourselves. I'm going up to my room to pack. It's been a lot of fun, but I'm ready to leave."

Micah was ready to leave as well and looked forward to going home to chill for a while. He glanced over at Kalina, deciding he wouldn't ask her about her decision again. He'd made it pretty clear he wanted her to spend her time off with him.

He glanced over at her while she stood to gather up her belongings. He couldn't stop his gaze from warming with pleasure as he watched her. Kalina Daniels had the ability to turn him on without even trying. His response to her had set off warning bells inside his head in Sydney, and those same bells were going off now.

He hadn't taken heed then, and he wouldn't be taking heed now.

He wanted her. Yes, she had hurt him by believing the worst, but he was willing to overlook that hurt because he had been partially to blame. He hadn't given her the opportunity to really get to know him. Now, he was offering her that chance, but it was something she had to want to do. So far, she didn't appear to know if she wanted to make that effort.

"I'm glad I was able to draw that blood and have it shipped to Washington before the Indian government stepped in," he heard her say.

He nodded as he stood. "I'm glad, as well. Hopefully, they'll be able to find something we couldn't."

"I hope so."

He studied her for a moment. "So, what are your plans for the evening?" Because of what she'd said that morning, he didn't want to ask specifically about dinner.

She drew in a deep breath. "Not sure. I just might decide to stay in with a good book."

"All right."

He fought back the desire to suggest they stay in together. Regardless of what they'd shared last night and this morning, Kalina would have to invite him to share any more time with her. The decision had to be hers…but there was nothing wrong with making sure she made the right one.

"I'm renting a car and going for a drive later," he offered.

She glanced over at him. "Really? Where?"

"No place in particular. I just need to get away from the villa for a while." He felt that they both did. Although they would be leaving India in a couple of days, they had pretty much stayed on the premises during the entire investigation. "You're invited to come with me if you'd like."

He could tell by her expression that she wanted to but was hesitant to accept his invitation. He wouldn't push. "Well, I'll see you later."

He had almost made it to the door, when she called after him. "Micah, if you're sure you don't mind having company, I'll tag alone."

Inwardly, he released a sigh of relief. He slowly turned to her. "No, I wouldn't mind. I would love having you with me. And there's a club I plan to check out, so put on your dancing shoes." Then without saying anything else, he walked out of the room.

Dancing shoes?

She shook her head recalling Micah's suggestion as she moved around her room at the villa. She loved dancing, but she'd never known him to dance. At least he'd never danced with her during those two months they'd been together. Even the night they'd met, at the ball. Other guys had asked her to dance, but Micah had not.

Micah had a lean, muscular physique, and she could imagine his body moving around on anyone's dance floor. So far, that had been something she hadn't seen. But she had been more than satisfied with all his moves in the bedroom and couldn't have cared less if any of those moves ever made it to the dance floor.

She heard a knock at the door, and her breath caught. Even with the distance separating them, she could feel the impact of his presence. After making love that morning, he had left her room to go to his and dress. They had met downstairs for breakfast with Theo. Today had been their last day at the lab. Tomorrow was a free day to do whatever they wanted, and then on Friday they would be flying out.

Major Harris had already called twice, asking where she wanted to go after she returned to Washington, and Kalina still wasn't certain she wanted to join Micah in Denver.

She knew she'd have to decide soon.

She quickly moved toward the door and opened it. Micah's slow perusal of her outfit let her know she'd done the right thing in wearing this particular dress. She had purchased it sometime last year at a boutique in Atlanta while visiting a college friend.

"You look nice," he said, giving her an appreciative smile.

She let her gaze roam over him and chuckled. "So do you. Come in for a moment. You're a little early, and I haven't switched out purses."

"No problem. Take your time."

Micah followed her into a sitting area and took the wingback chair she offered. When she left the room, he glanced around at the pictures on the wall. They were different from the ones in his room. His cousin Gemma was an interior decorator, and while taking classes at the university, she had decorated most of her family members' homes for practice. He would be the first to admit she'd done a good job. No one had been disappointed. He had been home for a short visit while she'd decorated his place, and she had educated him about what to look for in a painting when judging if it would fit the decor.

He was sure these same paintings had been on the wall when he'd carried Kalina through here in his arms last night. But his mind had been so preoccupied with getting her to bed, he hadn't paid any attention.

"I'm ready. Sorry to make you wait."

He glanced around, smiled and came to his feet. "No problem."

For a moment, neither of them said anything, but just stood there and stared at each other. Then finally he said, "I'm not going to pretend last night and this morning didn't happen, Kal."

She nodded slowly. "I don't recall asking you to."

She was right, she hadn't. "Good, then I guess it's safe for me to do this, since I've been dying to all day."

He reached out, tugged her closer to him and lowered his mouth to hers.

The arms that encompassed Kalina in an embrace were warm and protective. And the hand that rubbed up and down her spine was gentle.

But nothing could compare to the mouth that was taking her over with slow, deep, measured strokes. Already, desire was racing through her, and she couldn't do anything but moan her pleasure. No other two tongues could mate like theirs could, and she enjoyed the feel of his tongue in her mouth.

He shifted his stance to bring them closer, and she felt his hard erection pressing into her. It wouldn't bother her in the least if he were to suggest they stay in for the evening.

Instead, he finally broke contact, but immediately placed a quick kiss on her lips. "I love your taste," he whispered hotly.

She smiled up at him. "And I love yours, too."

The grin he shot her was naughty. "I'm going to have to keep that in mind."

She chuckled as she saw the glint of mischief in his gaze. "Yes, you do that."

Kalina always thought she could handle just about anything or anyone, but an hour or so after they'd left her room, she wasn't sure. She was seeing a side of Micah she had never seen before. It had started with the drive around the countryside. There had been just enough daylight left to enjoy the beauty of the section of town they hadn't yet seen, especially the shops situated at the foot of the Himalayas.

They had dined at a restaurant in the shopping district, and the food had been delicious. Now they were at the nightclub the restaurant manager had recommended.

She was in Micah's arms on the dance floor. The music was slow, and he was holding her while their bodies moved together in perfect rhythm. She was vaguely aware of their surroundings. The inside of the club was dark and crowded. Evidently this was a popular hangout. The servers were moving at a hurried pace to fill mixed-drink orders. And the live band rotated periodically with a deejay.

"I like this place, Micah. Thanks for bringing me here."

"You're welcome."

"And this is our first dance," she added.

He glanced down at her, tightened his arms around her and smiled. "I hope it's not our last."

She hoped that, as well. She liked the feel of being held by him in a place other than the bedroom. It felt good. But she could tell he wanted her from the hard bulge pressing against her whenever their bodies moved together. She liked the feel of it. She liked knowing she was desired. She especially appreciated knowing she could do that to him—even here in a crowded nightclub in the middle of a dance floor.

"Excalibur."

She glanced up at him. "Excuse me."

"My middle name is Excalibur."

She blinked, wondering why he was telling her that. "Oh, okay."

He chuckled. "You didn't know that, did you?"

She shrugged. "Was I supposed to?"

"I wish you had. I should have told you. We were involved for two months."

Yes, they had been involved, but their affair had been more about sex than conversation. He interrupted her thoughts by saying, "I know more about you than you know about me, Kalina."

She tilted her head to the side and looked at him. "You think so?"

"Yes."

"Well, then, tell me what you know," she said.

He tightened his arms around her waist as they swayed their bodies in time with the music. "You're twenty-seven. Your middle name is Marie. Your birthday is June fifteenth. Your favorite color is red. You hate eating beets. Your mother's name was Yvonne, and she died of cancer when you were ten."

He grinned as if proud of himself. "So what does that tell you?"

She stared at him for a few moments as if collecting her thoughts and then said, "I did more pillow talk than you did."

He laughed at that. "Sort of. What it tells me is that you shared more of yourself with me than I did with you."

They had already concluded there were a lot of things they didn't know about each other. So, okay, he had a heads-up on her information. That was fine. What they'd shared for those two months was a bed and not much else.

"It should not have been just sex between us, Kalina. I can see that now."

Now, *that's* where she disagreed. Their affair was never intended to be about anything but sex. For those two months, they had gotten to know each other intimately but not intellectually, and that's the way they'd wanted it. "If what you say is true, Micah, nobody told me. I distinctively recall you laying down the rules for a no-strings affair. And I remember agreeing to those rules. Your career was your life, and so was mine."

Evidently, she'd given him something to think about, because he didn't say anything to that. The music stopped, and he led her back to their table. A server was there, ready to take their drink order. One thing she'd noticed, two years ago and today, was that Micah was always a gentleman. He was a man who held doors open for ladies, who stood when women entered the room and who pulled out chairs for his date…the way he was doing now. "Thanks."

"You're welcome."

She glanced across the table at him. "You have impeccable manners."

He chuckled. "I wouldn't go that far, but I do my best."

"Do your brothers and cousins all have good manners like you?"

He winked. "Come home to Denver with me and find out."

Kalina rolled her eyes in exasperation. "You won't give up, will you?"

"No. I think you owe me the chance to clear my name."

He didn't say anything for a moment, allowing the server to place their drinks in front of them. Then she took a sip of her wine and asked, "Is clearing your name important to you, Micah?"

Leaning back, he stared over at her before saying, "If you really knew me the way I want you to know me, you wouldn't be asking me that."

She didn't say anything for a while. A part of her wanted to believe him, to believe that he truly did want her to get to know him better, to believe that he hadn't done what her father had said. But what if she went home with him, got to know him and, in the end, still felt he was capable to doing what she had accused him of doing?

"Micah—"

"You owe me that, Kalina. I think I've been more than fair, considering I am innocent of everything you've accused me of. Some men wouldn't give a damn about what you believed, but I do. Like I said, you owe me the chance to prove your father lied."

She drew in a deep breath. Did she owe him? She didn't have much time to think about it. He reached across the table and captured her small hand in his bigger one. Just a touch from him did things to her, made her feel what she didn't want to feel.

"I hadn't wanted to make love to you again until we resolved things between us," he said in a low tone.

She gave a cynical laugh. "So now you're going to claim making love last night and this morning was my idea?"

"No. I wanted you, and I knew that you wanted me."

He was right, and there was no need to ask how he'd known that. She had wanted him, and she'd been fully aware that he had wanted her.

"Would it make you feel more comfortable about going home with me if I promise not to touch you while you're there?"

She narrowed her gaze. "No, because all you'll do is find ways to tempt me to the point where I'll end up being the one seeking you out. I'm well aware of those games you play, Micah."

He didn't deny it. "Okay, then. We are adults," he said. "With needs. But the purpose of you going to Denver with me is not to continue our sexual interactions. I want to make that clear up front."

He had made that clear more times than she cared to count. Her stomach knotted, and she wondered when she would finally admit that the real reason she was reluctant to go to Denver was that she might end up getting too attached to him, to his family, to her surroundings…

Her heart hammered at the mere thought of that happening. For years, especially after her grandparents' deaths, she had felt like a loner. She'd had her father—whenever he managed to stay in one place long enough to be with her. But their relationship wasn't like most parent-child relationships. She believed deep down that he loved her, but she also knew that he expressed that

love by trying to control her. As long as she followed
his orders like one of his soldiers, she remained in his
good graces. But if she rebelled, there was hell to pay.
The only reason he had apologized for his actions regarding her canceled trip to Beijing was that, for the
first time in his life, he saw that he could make her
angry enough that he could lose her. She had been just
that upset with him, and he knew it. Although he had
never admitted it, her father was just as much of a mav-
erick as she was.

She glanced down at the table and saw that Micah
was still holding her hand. It felt good. Too good. Too
right. She thought about pulling her hand away, but decided to let it stay put since he seemed content holding
it. Her breathing quickened when he began stroking her
palm in a light caress. His touch was so stimulating it
played on her nerve endings as if they were the strings
of a well-tuned guitar.

She glanced up and met his gaze. He stopped stroking her skin and curved his hand over hers to entwine
their fingers. "No matter what you believe, Kal, I would
never intentionally hurt you."

She nodded and then he slowly withdrew his hand
from hers. She instantly felt the loss of that contact.

He glanced around the club and then at the dance
floor. The deejay was playing another slow song.
"Come on, I want to hold you in my arms again," he
said, reaching out and taking her hand one more time.

He led her to the dance floor, and she placed her
head on his chest. He wrapped his arms around her,
encompassing her in his embrace. His heart was beating fast against her cheek, and his erection pressed hard
against her middle again. She smiled. Did he really

think they could go to Denver together and not share a bed?

She chuckled. Now she was beginning to wonder if he really knew *her* that well.

He touched her chin and tipped her head back to meet his gaze. "You okay?"

She nodded, deciding not to tell him what she'd found so comical, especially since he was wearing such a serious expression on his face.

She saw something in the depths of his dark eyes that she didn't understand at first glance. But then she knew what she saw. It was a tenderness that was reaching out to her, making her feel both vulnerable and needed at the same time. At that moment she knew the truth.

"Kalina?"

The release of her name from his lips sent a shiver racing up her spine. Drawing in much-needed air, she said. "Yes, I'm fine. And I've reached a decision, Micah. I'm going to Denver with you."

Eight

"Welcome to Micah's Manor, Kalina,"

Micah stood aside as Kalina entered his home and looked around. He saw both awe and admiration reflected in her features. He hadn't told her what to expect and now he was glad that he hadn't. This was the first official visit to his place by any woman other than one of his relatives. What Kalina thought mattered to him.

In his great-grandfather's will, it had been declared that every Westmoreland heir would receive one hundred acres of land at the age of twenty-five. As the oldest, Dillon got the family homestead, which included the huge family house that sat on over three hundred acres.

Micah had already established a career as an epidemiologist and was living in Washington by the time his twenty-fifth birthday came around. For years, he'd kept the land undeveloped and whenever he came home he would crash at Dillon's place. But when Dillon got married and had a family of his own, Micah felt it was time to build his own house.

He had taken off six months to supervise the project. That had been the six months following the end of his affair with the very woman now standing in his living room. He had needed something to occupy his time, and his thoughts, and having this house built seemed the perfect project.

He could count on one finger the number of times he had actually spent the night here, since he rarely came home. The last time had been when he'd come to Denver for his brother Jason's wedding reception in August. It had been nice to stay at his own place, and the logistics had worked out fine since he, his siblings and cousins all had houses in proximity to each other.

"So, what do you think?" he asked, placing Kalina's luggage by the front door.

"This place is for one person?"

He couldn't help laughing. He knew why she was asking. Located at the south end of the rural area that the locals referred to as Westmoreland Country, Micah's Manor sat on Gemma Lake, the huge body of water his great-grandfather had named in honor of his wife when he'd settled here all those years ago. Micah's huge ranch-style house was three stories high with over six thousand square feet of living space.

"Yes. I admit I let Gemma talk me into getting carried away, but—"

"Gemma?"

"One of my cousins. She's an interior designer. To

take full advantage of the lake, she figured I needed the third floor, and as for the size, I figured when my time ended with the feds, I would want to settle down, marry and raise a family. It was easier to build that dream house now instead of adding on later."

"Good planning."

"I thought so at the time. I picked the plan I liked best, hired a builder and hung around for six months to make sure things got off to a good start," he added.

"Oh, I see."

He knew she really didn't. She had no idea that when he'd selected this particular floor plan he had envisioned her sharing it with him, even though the last thing she had uttered to him was that she hated his guts. For some reason, he hadn't been able to push away the fantasy that one day she would come here and see this place. He had even envisioned them making love in his bedroom while seeing the beauty of the lake. Having Kalina here now was a dream come true.

"I had to leave on assignment to Peru for a few months and when I returned, the house was nearly finished. I took more time off and was here when Gemma began decorating it."

"It is beautiful, Micah."

He was glad she liked it. "Thanks. I practically gave Gemma an open checkbook, and she did her thing. Of course, since it wasn't her money, she decided to splurge a little."

Kalina raised a dubious brow. "A little?"

He shrugged and grinned. "Okay, maybe a lot. Up until a year ago she used this place as a model home to showcase her work whenever she was trying to impress new clients. As you can see, her work speaks for itself."

Kalina glanced around. "Yes, it sure does. Your cousin is very gifted. Is she no longer in the business?"

"She's still in it."

"But she no longer needs your house as a model?" Kalina asked.

"No, mainly because she's living in Australia now that she and Callum are married. That's where he's from. They have a two-month-old son. You'll get to meet them some time next week. She's coming home for a visit."

He had given his family strict orders to stay away from his place to give him time to get settled in with his houseguest. Of course, everyone was anxious to meet the woman he'd brought home with him.

"This should be an interesting thirty days," she said, admiring a huge painting on the wall.

"Why do you say that?"

She shrugged. "Well, all those markers I saw getting here. Jason's Place. Zane's Hideout. Canyon's Bluff. Ramsey's Web. Derringer's Dungeon. Stern's Stronghold… Need I go on?"

He chuckled. "No, and you have my cousin Bailey to thank for that. We give her the honor of naming everyone's parcel of land, and she's come up with some doozies." He picked up her luggage. "Come on, I'll show you to your room. If you aren't in the mood to climb the stairs, I do have an elevator."

"No, the stairs are fine. Besides, it gives me the chance to work the kinks out of my body from our long flight."

She followed him to one of the guest rooms on the

third floor. They hadn't slept together since that one night he'd spent with her after they'd met on the staircase. Even after he'd taken her dancing, he had returned her to her room at the villa, planted a kiss on her cheek and left. The next day had been extremely busy with them packing up the lab's equipment and finalizing reports.

They had been too busy to spend time getting naked on silken sheets. But that hadn't meant the thought hadn't run through his mind a few times. Yesterday they'd taken the plane here, and sat beside each other for the flight. The twelve hours from India to Washington, and then the six hours from Washington to Denver had given him time to reflect on what he hoped she would get from her thirty days with him and his family.

"Wow!" Kalina walked into Micah's guest bedroom and couldn't do anything but stare, turn around and stare some more.

The room was done in chocolate, white and lime green. Everything—from the four-poster, white, queen-size bed, to the curtains and throw pillows—was perfectly matched. The walls of the room were painted white, which made the space look light and airy. Outside her huge window was a panoramic view of the lake she'd seen when they arrived. There was a private bath that was triple the size of the one she had in her home in Virginia. It had both a Jacuzzi tub and a walk-in shower.

She wasn't surprised Micah had given her one of his guest rooms to use. He wanted to shift their relationship from the physical to the mental. She just wasn't so sure she agreed with his logic. She could still get to know him while they shared a bed, and she didn't understand why he assumed differently. She watched him place the luggage by her bed. He said nothing as she continued to check out other interesting aspects of the room.

"I can see why Gemma used your house as a model home," Kalina said, coming to stand in front of him. "Your house should be featured in one of those magazines."

He chuckled. "It was. Last year. I have a copy downstairs. You can read the article if you like."

"All right."

"I'll leave you to rest up and relax. I plan on preparing dinner later."

She raised a surprised brow. "You can cook?"

He laughed. "Of course I can cook. And I'm pretty good at it, you'll see." He reached out and softly kissed her on the lips. "Now, get some rest."

He turned to leave, but she stopped him. "Where's your room?"

He smiled down at her as if he had an idea why she was asking. "It's on the second floor. I'll give you a tour of my bedroom anytime you want it."

She nodded, fully aware that a tour of his bedroom wasn't what she was really interested in. She wanted to try out his bed.

A few hours later, Kalina closed her eyes as she savored the food in her mouth. "Mmm, this is delicious," she said, slowly opening her eyes and glancing across the dinner table at Micah.

After indulging in a bath in the Jacuzzi, she had taken a nap, only to awaken hours later to the smell of something good cooking in the kitchen downstairs. She had slipped into a T-shirt and a pair of capris, and, not bothering to put shoes on, she had headed downstairs to find Micah at the stove. In his bare feet, shirtless, with jeans riding low on his hips, he'd looked the epitome of sexy as he moved around his spacious kitchen. She had watched him and had seen for herself just how at home he was while making a meal. She couldn't help admiring him. Some men couldn't even boil water.

He had told her he could cook, but she hadn't taken him at his word. Now, after tasting what he'd prepared, she was forced to believe him. *Almost.* She glanced around the kitchen.

"What are you looking for?" he asked her.

She looked back at him and smiled. "Your chef."

Micah chuckled. "You won't find one here. I did all this myself. I don't particularly like cooking, but I won't starve if I have to do it for myself."

No, he wouldn't starve. In fact, he had enough cooking skills to keep himself well fed. He had prepared meat loaf, rice and gravy, green beans and iced tea. He'd explained that he'd called ahead and had gotten his cousin Megan to go grocery shopping for him. She'd picked up everything he'd asked her to get and a few things he hadn't asked her for…like the three flavors of ice cream now in the freezer.

"Do you ever get lonely out here, Micah?"

He glanced across the table at her and laughed. "Are you kidding? I have relatives all around me. I try to catch up on my rest whenever I'm home, but they don't make it easy. Although I'm not here the majority of the time, I'm involved in the family business. I have a share in my brother's and cousins' horse-breeding business, in my cousin Ramsey's sheep business and I'm on the board of Blue Ridge Land Management." He then told her how his father and uncle had founded the company years ago and how his brother Dillon was now CEO.

Kalina immediately recognized the name of the company. It had made the Forbes Top 50 just this year. She could only sit and stare at him. She'd had no idea he was one of *those* Westmorelands.

Not that having a lot of money was everything, but it told her more about his character than he realized. He worked because he wanted to work, not because he had to. Yet he always worked just as hard as any member of his team—sometimes even harder. She couldn't help wondering how he'd chosen his field of work and why he was so committed and dedicated to it.

Over dinner he told her more about his family, his brothers and cousins, especially the escapades of the younger Westmorelands. Although she tried not to laugh, she found some of their antics downright comical and could only imagine how his cousins Dillon and Ramsey had survived it all while still managing to keep the family together.

"And you say there are fifteen of you?" she asked, pushing her plate away.

"Yes, of the Denver clan. Everyone is here except Gemma, who now lives in Sydney, and the few who are still away at college. Needless to say, the holidays are fun times for us when everyone comes home."

Getting up to take their plates to the sink, he asked, "Do you feel like going horseback riding later? I thought I'd give you a tour of the rest of the house and then we can ride around my property."

Excitement spread through her. "I'd like that."

He returned to the seat next to her. "But first I think we need to have a talk."

She lifted an eyebrow. "About what?"

"About whose bed you'll be sleeping in while you're here."

And before she could respond, he had swept her out of her chair and into his arms. He carried her from the kitchen into the living room where he settled down on the sofa with her in his lap.

Micah smiled at the confused look on Kalina's face. She brushed back a handful of hair and then pinned him with one of her famous glares. "I didn't know there was a question about where I'd be sleeping."

She wasn't fooling him one bit. "Isn't there? I put you in the guest room for a reason."

She waved off his words. "Then maybe we do need to talk about that foolishness regarding your no-sex policy again."

He'd figured she would want to discuss it, which was why he'd brought up the subject. "It will be less complicated if we don't share the same bed for a while."

"Until I really get to know you?"

"Yes."

"I disagree with your logic on taking that approach, especially since you want me. Do you deny it?"

How could he deny it when he had an erection he knew she could feel since she was practically sitting on it. "No, I don't deny it, but like I said when I invited you here, I want you to—"

"Get to know you," she muttered. "I heard you. More times than I care to. And I don't think us sharing a bed has anything to do with what we do outside the bedroom."

"Well, I do. Last time we had an affair it was strictly

sexual. Now I want to change the way you think about me, about us."

Now she really looked confused. "To what?"

He wished he could tell her the truth, that she was the woman he wanted above all others. That he wanted to marry her. He wanted her to have his babies. He wanted her to wear his name. But all the things he wanted meant nothing until she could trust him. They would never come into existence until she could believe he was not the man her father had made him out to be. This time around, Micah refused to allow sex to push those wants to the side.

"I want you to think of things other than sex when it comes to us, Kalina," he said.

She frowned. "Why?"

He could come clean and tell her how he felt about her, but he didn't think she would believe him, just as she still didn't believe he had not betrayed her two years ago. "Because we've been there before. Even you said that our relationship was starting with the same technique. I want you to feel that it's different this time."

He could tell she still didn't know where he was coming from, but the important thing was that *he* knew. A dawning awareness suddenly appeared on her features, but he had a feeling, even before she opened her mouth, that whatever she was thinking was all wrong.

"Okay, I think I get it," she said, nodding.

He was afraid to ask, but knew he had to. "And just what do you get?"

"You're one of the older Westmorelands and you feel you should set an example for the others." She nodded her head as if her assumption made perfect sense.

"Set an example for them in what way?" he asked.

"By presenting me as a friend and not a lover. You did say your cousin Bailey was young and impressionable."

He had to keep a straight face. He forced his eyes to stay focused even though he was tempted to roll them. Once she met Bailey she would see how absurd her assumption was. First of all, although she was twenty-three years old, Bailey probably didn't have much of a love life, thanks to all her older, overbearing and protective brothers and male cousins. And she had gone past being impressionable. Bailey could curse worse than any sailor when she put her mind to it. He and his brothers and cousins had already decided that the man who fell for Bailey would have to be admired...as well as pitied.

"The key word where Bailey is concerned is *was*. Trust me. I don't have to hide my affairs from anyone. Everyone around here is an adult and understands what grown-ups do."

"In that case, what other reason could you have for not wanting us to sleep together? Unless..."

He stared at her for several long moments, and when she didn't finish what she was about to say, he prompted her. "Unless what?"

She looked down at her hands in her lap. "Nothing."

He had a feeling that again, whatever was bothering her, she'd figured wrong. He reached out, lifted her chin up and brought his face closer to hers. "And I know good and well you aren't thinking what I think you're thinking, not when my desire for you is about to burst through my zipper. There's no way you can deny that you feel it."

She nodded slowly. "Yes, I can feel it," she said softly.

So could he, and he was aware, even more than he'd been before, of just how much he wanted her. Unfortunately, pointing out his body's reaction made her aware of how much he wanted her, as well.

She stuck her tongue out and slowly licked the corner of his lips. "Then why are you denying me what I want? Why are you denying yourself what you want?"

Good question. He had to think hard to recall the reason he was denying them both. He had a plan. A little sacrifice now would pay off plenty of dividends in the years to come. Remembering his goals wouldn't have been so hard if she hadn't decided at that very moment to play the vixen. She purposely twisted that little behind of hers in his lap, against his zipper, making him mindful of just how good his erection felt against her backside. And what the hell was she doing with her tongue, using the tip of it to lick his mouth? She was deliberately boggling his mind.

"Kalina?"

"Mmm?"

"Stop it," he said in a tone he knew was not really strong on persuasion. It wasn't helping matters that he'd once fantasized about them making love in this very room and on this very sofa.

"No, I don't want to stop and you can't make me," she said in that stubborn voice of hers.

Hell, okay, he silently agreed. *Maybe I can't make her stop.* And he figured that reasoning with her would be a waste of time....

At that moment she moved her tongue lower to lick the area around his jaw and he groaned.

"Oh, I so love the way you taste, Micah."

Those were the wrong words for her to say. Hearing them made him recall just how much he loved how she tasted, as well. He drew in a deep breath, hoping to find resistance. Instead, he inhaled her feminine scent, a telltale sign of how much she wanted him. He could just imagine the sweetness of her nectar.

He thought of everything…counting sheep, the pictures on the wall, the fact that he hadn't yet cleaned off the kitchen table…but nothing could clear his mind of her scent, or the way she was using her tongue. Now she had moved even lower to lick around his shoulder blades. Hell, why hadn't he put on a shirt?

"Baby, you've got to stop," he urged her in a strained voice.

She ignored him and kept right on doing what she was doing. He tried giving himself a mental shake and found it did not work. She was using her secret weapon, that blasted tongue of hers, to break him down. Hell, he would give anything for something—even a visit from one of his kin—to interrupt what she was doing, because he was losing the willpower to put a stop to it.

Hot, achy sensations swirled in his gut when she scooted off his lap. By the time he had figured out what she was about to do, it was too late. She had slid down his zipper and reached inside his jeans to get just what she wanted. He tightened his arms on her, planning to pull her up, but again he was too late. She lowered her head and took him into her mouth.

Kalina ignored the tug on her hair and kept her mouth firmly planted on Micah. By the time she was finished with him, he would think twice about resisting her, not giving her what she wanted or acting on foolish thoughts like them not sharing a bed now that she'd come all the way to Denver with him. He had a lot of nerve.

And he had a lot of this, she thought, fitting her mouth firmly on him, barely able to do so because he was so large. He was the only man she'd ever done this to. The first time she hadn't been sure she had done it correctly. But he had assured her that she had, and he'd also assured her he had enjoyed it immensely. So she might as well provide him with more enjoyment, maybe then he would start thinking the way she wanted him to. Or, for the moment, stop thinking at all.

"Damn, Kalina, please stop."

She heard his plea, but thought it didn't sound all that convincing, so she continued doing what she was doing, and pretty soon the tug on her hair stopped. Now he was twirling her locks around his fingers to hold her mouth in place. No need. She didn't intend to go anywhere.

At least she thought she wouldn't be. Suddenly, he pulled her up and tossed her down on the sofa. The moment her back hit the cushions he was there, lifting her T-shirt over her head and sliding her capris and panties down her legs, leaving her totally naked.

The heat of his gaze raked over her, and she felt it everywhere, especially in her feminine core. "No need to let a good erection go to waste, Micah," she said saucily.

He evidently agreed with her. Tugging his jeans and briefs down over his muscular hips, he didn't waste any time slipping out of the clothes before moving to take his place between her open legs.

She lifted her arms to receive him and whispered, "Just think of this as giving me a much-deserved treat."

Kalina would have laughed at his snort if he hadn't captured her mouth in his the moment he slid inside her, not stopping until he went all the way to the hilt. And then he began moving inside her, stroking her desire to the point of raging out of control. She lifted her hips off the sofa to receive every hard thrust. The wall of his chest touched hers, brushing against her breasts in a rhythm that sent sensations rushing through her bloodstream.

Then he pulled away from her mouth, looked down at her and asked in a guttural voice, "Why?"

She knew what he was asking. "Because it makes no sense to deny us this pleasure."

He didn't say whether he agreed with her or not. Instead, he placed his hands against her backside and lifted her hips so they would be ready to meet his downward plunge. She figured he probably wasn't happy with her. He wouldn't appreciate how she had tempted him and pushed him over the edge. She figured he would stew for a while, but that was fine. Eventually he would get over it.

But apparently not before he put one sensuous whipping on her, she thought, loving the feel of how he was moving inside her. It was as if he wanted to use his body to give her a message, but she wasn't sure just what point he was trying to make. She reached up and cupped his face in her hands, forcing him to look at her. "What?" she asked breathlessly.

He started to move his lips in reply, but then, instead, leaned down and captured her mouth in his, leaving her wondering what he had been about to say. Probably just another scolding. All thoughts left her mind when she got caught up in his kiss and the way he was stroking inside her body.

She dropped her hands to his shoulders and then wrapped her arms around his neck as every sensation intensified. Then her body exploded, and simultaneously, so did his. They cried out each other's names.

This, she concluded, as a rush swept over her, was pleasure beyond anything they'd shared before. This was worth his irritation once everything was over. For now, she was fueled by this. She was stroked, claimed and overpowered by the most sensuous lovemaking she had ever known. By Micah's hands and his body.

This had been better than any fantasy, and she couldn't think of a better way to be welcomed to Micah's Manor.

Nine

Okay, so she hadn't held a gun to his head or forced him to make love to her, but he was still pissed. Not only at her but at himself, Micah concluded the next morning as he walked out of the house toward the barn.

After they'd made love yesterday, Kalina had passed out. He had gathered her in his arms and taken her up the stairs to the guest room. After placing her naked body beneath the covers, he had left, closing the door behind him. He'd even thought about locking it. The woman was dangerous. She had not been so rebellious the last time.

Cursing and calling himself all kinds of names—including whipped, weakling and fickle—he had cleaned up the kitchen, unpacked his luggage and done some laundry. By the time he'd finished all his chores, it had gotten dark outside. He'd then gone into his office and made calls to his family to let them know he'd returned. Most had figured as much when they'd seen lights burning over at his place. He had again warned them that he didn't want to be disturbed. He'd assured them that he and his houseguest would make an appearance when they got good and ready. He ended up agreeing to bring her to dinner tomorrow night at the big house.

By the time he'd hung up the phone after talking to everyone, it was close to nine o'clock and he was surprised that he hadn't heard a peep out of Kalina. He checked on her and found her still sleeping. He had left her that way, figuring that when she'd caught up on her rest she would wake up. Still angry with himself for giving in to temptation and momentarily forgetting his plan, he'd gone to bed.

He'd awakened around midnight to the sound of footsteps coming down the stairs. He was very much aware when the footsteps paused in front of his closed bedroom door before finally progressing to the first floor. He had flipped onto his back and listened to the sound of Kalina moving around downstairs, knowing she was raiding his refrigerator—probably getting into those three flavors of ice cream.

When he had woken up this morning he had checked on her again. Sometime during the night she had changed into a pair of pajamas and was now sleeping on top of the covers. It had taken everything within him not to shed his own clothes and slide into that bed beside her.

Then he'd gotten mad at himself for thinking he should not have let her sleep alone. He should have made love to her all through the night. He should have let her go to sleep in his arms. He should have woken her up with his lovemaking this morning.

He had quickly forced those thoughts from his mind, considering them foolish, and had gone into the kitchen. He had prepared breakfast and kept it warming on the stove for her while he headed to the barn. He preferred not to be around when she woke up. The woman was pure temptation and making love to her every chance he got was not what he had in mind for this trip.

He had thought about getting into his truck and going to visit his family, but knew it wouldn't be a good idea to be off the property when Kalina finally woke up. He glanced at his watch. It was nine o'clock already. Was she planning to sleep until noon? His family probably figured he was keeping them away because he didn't want them to invade his private time with her. Boy, were they wrong.

"Good morning, Micah. I'm ready to go riding now."

He spun around and stared straight into Kalina's face. "Where did you come from?"

She smiled and looked at him as if he'd asked a silly question. "From inside the house. Where else would I have been?"

He frowned. "I didn't hear you approach."

She used her hand to wave off his words. "Whatever. You promised to take me riding yesterday, but we didn't get around to it since we were indulging in other things. I'm ready now."

His frown deepened, knowing just what those "other things" were. She was dressed in a pair of well-worn jeans, boots and a button-down shirt. He tried not to stare so hard at how the jeans fit her body, making him want to caress each of her curves. She looked good, and it took everything he had to keep his eyes from popping out of their sockets.

"Are we going riding or not?"

He glanced up at her face and saw her chin had raised a fraction. She expected a fight and was evidently ready for one. Just as she had been ready for them to make love yesterday. Well, he had news for her. Unlike yesterday, he wouldn't be accommodating her.

"Fine," he said, grabbing his Stetson off a rack on the barn wall. "Let's ride."

Kalina couldn't believe Micah was in a bad mood just because she had tempted him into making love to her. But here they were, riding side by side, and he was all but ignoring her.

She glanced over at him when he brought the horses to a stop along a ridge so she could look down over the valley. His Stetson was pulled low on his brow, and the shadow on his chin denoted he hadn't shaved that morning. He wore a dark brooding look, but, in her opinion, he appeared so sexy, so devastatingly handsome, that it was a total turn-on. It had taken all she could not to suggest they return to his place and make love. With his present mood, she knew better than to push her luck.

"Any reason you're staring at me, Kal?"

She inwardly smiled. So…he'd known she was looking. "No reason. I was just thinking."

He glanced over at her, tipped his hat back and those bedroom-brown eyes sent sensations floating around in her stomach. "Thinking about what?"

"Your mood. Are you typically a moody person?"

He frowned and looked back at the valley. "I'm not moody," he muttered.

"Yes, you are. Sex puts most men in a good mood. I see it does the opposite for you. I find that pretty interesting."

He glanced back at her. A tremor coursed through her with the look he was giving her. It was hot, regardless of the reason. "You just don't get it, do you?"

She shrugged. "Evidently not, so how about enlightening me on what I just don't get."

He inhaled deeply and then muttered, "Nothing."

"Evidently there is something, Micah."

He looked away again and moments later looked back at her. "There is nothing."

He then glanced at his watch. "I promised everyone I would bring you to dinner at the big house. They can hardly wait to meet you."

"And I'm looking forward to meeting them, too."

He watched her for a long moment. Too long. "What?" she asked, wondering why he kept staring at her.

He shook his head. "Nothing. I promised you a tour of the place. Come on. Let's go back home."

It was only moments later, as they rode side by side, that it dawned on her what he'd said.

"Let's go back home..."

Although she knew Micah hadn't meant it the way it had sounded, he'd said it as if they were a married couple and Micah's Manor was theirs. Something pricked inside her. Why was she suddenly feeling disappointed at the thought that Micah's home would never be hers?

* * *

"I like Kalina, Micah, and she's nothing like I expected."

Micah took a sip of his drink as he stood with Zane on the sidelines, watching how his female cousins and cousins-in-law had taken Kalina into their midst and were making her feel right at home. He could tell from the smile on Kalina's face that she was comfortable around them.

Micah glanced up at his cousin. "What were you expecting?"

Zane chuckled. "Another mad scientist like you. Someone who was going to bore us with all that scientific mumbo jumbo. I definitely wasn't expecting a sexy doctor. Hell, if she didn't belong to you, I would hit on her myself."

Micah couldn't help smiling. He, of all people, knew about his cousin's womanizing ways. "I'm sure you would, and I'm glad you're not. I appreciate the loyalty."

"No problem. But you might want to lay down the law to the twins when they arrive next week."

He thought about his twin cousins, Aidan and Adrian, and the trouble they used to get into—the trouble they could still get into at times although both were away at college and doing well. It was something about being in Westmoreland Country that made them want to revert to being hellions—especially when it came to women.

"You haven't brought a woman home for us to meet since Patrice. Does this mean anything?"

Micah took another sip of his drink before deciding to be completely honest. "I plan to marry Kalina one day."

A smooth smile touched Zane's features. "Figured as much. Does she know it?"

"Not yet. I'm trying to give her the chance to get to know me."

If Zane found that comment strange he didn't let on. Instead, he changed the subject and brought Micah up to date on how things were going in the community. Micah listened, knowing that if anyone knew what was going on it would be Zane.

Micah was well aware that Westmoreland Country would become a madhouse in a few weeks, when everyone began arriving for the christening of Gemma's baby. They were expecting all those other Westmorelands from Atlanta, Texas and Montana. And his brothers and cousins attending college had planned to return for the event, as well.

"I hadn't heard Dillon say whether Bane is coming home."

Zane shrugged. "Not sure since he might be in training someplace."

Micah nodded. Everyone knew of his baby brother's quest to become a Navy SEAL, as well as Bane's mission to one day find the woman he'd given up a few years ago. And knowing his brother as he did, Micah knew Brisbane would eventually succeed in doing both.

"I like Kalina, Micah."

Micah turned when his brother Jason walked up. The most recent member of the family to marry, Jason and his wife, Bella, were expecting twins. From the look of Bella, the babies would definitely arrive any day now.

"I'm glad you do since you might as well get used to seeing her around," Micah said.

"Does that mean you're thinking of retiring as the

Westmoreland mad scientist and returning home to start a family?" Jason asked.

Micah chuckled. "No, it doesn't mean any of that. I love my career, and Kalina loves hers. It just means we'll be working together more, and whenever I come home we'll come together."

He took a sip of his drink, thinking that what he'd just said sounded really good. Now all he had to do was convince Kalina. She had to get to know the real him, believe in him, trust him and then they could move on in their lives together.

He still wasn't happy about the stunt she'd pulled on him yesterday. He was determined to keep his distance until she realized the truth about him.

Kalina glanced across the room at Micah before turning her attention back to the women surrounding her. All of them had gone out of their way to make her feel at home. She hadn't known what to expect from this family dinner, but the one thing she hadn't expected was to find a group of women who were so warm and friendly.

Even Bailey, who Micah had said had been standoffish to Patrice, was more than friendly, and Kalina felt the warm hospitality was genuine. She readily accepted the women's invitation to go shopping with them later this week and to do other things like take in a couple of chick flicks, visit the spa and get their hair done. They wanted to have a "fun" week. Given Micah's present mood, she figured spending time away from him wouldn't be a bad idea.

After they'd returned to the ranch from riding, he had taken her on a quick tour of his home. Just like yesterday, she had been more than impressed with what she'd seen. His bedroom had left her speechless, and she couldn't imagine him sleeping in that huge bed alone. She planned to remedy that. It made no sense for them to be sleeping in separate beds. He wouldn't be happy about it, but he would just have to get over it.

"Um, I wonder what has Micah frowning," Pam Westmoreland, Dillon's wife, leaned over to whisper to her. "He keeps looking over this way, and I recognize that look. It's one of those Westmoreland 'you're not doing as I say' looks."

Kalina couldn't help smiling. The woman who was married to the oldest Westmoreland here had pegged her brother-in-law perfectly. "He's stewing over something I did, but he'll get over it."

Pam chuckled. "Yes, eventually he will. Once in a while they like to have their way but don't think we should have ours. There's nothing wrong with showing them that 'their way' isn't always the best way."

Hours later, while sitting beside Micah as he drove them back to Micah's Manor, Kalina recalled the conversation she'd had with Pam. Maybe continuing to defy his expectations—showing him that his way wasn't the best way—was how she should continue to handle Micah.

"Did you enjoy yourself, Kalina?"

She glanced over at him. He hadn't said much to her all evening, although the only time he'd left her side was when the women had come to claim her. If this was his way of letting her get to know him then he was way off the mark.

"Yes, I had a wonderful time. I enjoyed conversing

with the women in your family. They're all nice. I like them."

"They like you, too. I could tell."

"What about you, Micah? Do you like me?"

He seemed surprised by her question. "Yes, of course. Why do you ask?"

"Um, no reason."

She looked straight ahead at the scenery flying by the car's windshield, and felt a warm sensation ignite within her every time she was aware that he was looking at her.

She surprised him when she caught him staring one of those times. Just so he wouldn't know she was onto what he was doing, she smiled and asked, "Was your grandfather Raphel really married to all those women? Bailey told me the story of how he became the black sheep of the family after running off in the early 1900s with the preacher's wife and about all the other wives he supposedly collected along the way."

Micah made a turn into Micah's Manor. "That's what everyone wants to find out. We need to know if there are any more Westmorelands out there that we don't know about. That's how we found out about our cousins living in Atlanta, Montana and Texas. Until a few years ago, we were unaware that Raphel had a twin by the name of Reginald Westmoreland. He's the great-grandfather for those other Westmorelands. Megan is hiring a private detective to help solve the puzzle about Raphel's other wives. We've eliminated two as having given birth to heirs, and now we have two more to check out."

He paused a moment and said, "The investigator, a guy by the name of Rico Claiborne, was to start work on the case months ago, but his involvement in another case has delayed things for a while. We're hoping he can start the search soon. Megan is determined to see how many more Westmorelands she can dig up."

Kalina chuckled. "There are so many of you now. I can't imagine there being others."

Micah smiled. "Well, there are, trust me. You'll get to meet them in a few weeks when they arrive for Gemma and Callum's son's christening."

"Must be nice," she said softly.

He glanced over at her. "What must be?"

"To be part of a big family where everyone is close and looks out for each other. I like that. I've never experienced anything like that before. Other than my grandparents, there has only been me and Dad…and well, you know how my relationship with him is most of the time."

Micah didn't say anything, and maybe it was just as well. It didn't take much for Kalina to recall what had kept them apart for the past two years. Although he was probably hoping otherwise, by getting to know him better, all she'd seen so far was his moody side.

When he brought the car to a stop, she said, "You like having your way, don't you, Micah?"

He didn't say anything at first and then he pushed his Stetson back out of his face. "Is that what you think?"

"Yes. But maybe you should consider something?"

"What?"

"Whatever it is you're trying to prove to me, there's a possibility that your way isn't the best way to prove it. You brought me here so I could get to know you better. It's day two and already we're at odds with each other, and only because I tempted you into doing something that I knew we both wanted to do anyway. But if you prefer that it not happen again, then it won't. In other words, I will give you just what you want…which is practically nothing."

Without saying anything else, she opened the door, got out of the truck and walked toward the house.

Be careful what you ask for, Micah thought over his cup of coffee a few mornings later as he watched Kalina enter the kitchen. She'd been here for five days. Things between them weren't bad, but they could be better. It wasn't that they were mad at each other. In fact, they were always pleasant to each other. Too pleasant.

She had no idea that beneath all his pleasantry was a man who was horny as hell. A man whose body ached to make love to her, hold her at night. He wished she could sleep with him instead of sleeping alone in his guest bedroom. But his mind knew his decision that he and Kalina not make love for a while was the right one to make. It was his body wishing things could be different.

They would see each other in the mornings, and then usually, during the day, they went their separate ways. It wasn't uncommon for one of his female cousins or cousins-in-laws to come pick her up. On those days, he wouldn't see her till much later. So much for them spending time together.

"Good morning, Micah."

He put down his cup and pushed the newspaper aside. "Good morning, Kalina. Did you enjoy going shopping yesterday?"

She sat down at the table across from him and smiled. "I didn't go shopping yesterday. We did that two days ago. Yesterday, we went into town and watched a movie. One of those chick flicks."

He nodded. She could have asked him, and he would have taken her to the movies, chick flick or not. He got up to pour himself another cup of coffee, trying not to notice what she was wearing. Most days she would be wearing jeans and a top. Today she had put on a simple dress. Seeing her in it reminded him once again of what a nice pair of legs she owned.

"Are you and the ladies going someplace again today?" he decided to ask her.

She shook her head. "No. I plan to hang around here today. But I promise not to get in your way."

"You won't get in my way." He came back to the table and sat down. "Other than that day we went riding, I haven't shown you the rest of my property."

She lifted an eyebrow in surprise. "You mean there's more?"

He chuckled. "Yes, there's a part that I lease out to Ramsey for his sheep, and then another part I lease out to my brother Jason and my cousins Zane and Derringer for their horse-breeding business."

He took a sip of his coffee. "So how about us spending the day together?"

She smiled brightly. "I'd love to."

Hours later when Micah and Kalina returned to Micah's Manor, she dropped down in the first chair she came to, which was a leather recliner in the living room. When Micah had suggested they spend time together, she hadn't expected that they would be gone for most of the day.

First, after she had changed clothes, they had gone

riding and he'd shown her the rest of his property. Then he had come back so they could change clothes, and they had taken the truck into town. He had driven to the nursing home to visit a man by the name of Henry Ryan. Henry, Micah had explained, had been the town's doctor for years and had delivered every Westmoreland born in Denver, including his parents. The old man, who was in his late nineties, was suffering from a severe case of Alzheimer's.

It had been obvious to Kalina from the first that the old man had been glad to see Micah and vice versa. Today, Henry's mind appeared sharp, and he had shared a lot with her, including some stories from Micah's childhood years. On the drive home, Micah had explained that things weren't always that way. There would be days when he visited Henry and the old man hadn't known who he was. Micah had credited Henry with being the one to influence him to go into the medical field.

Today, Kalina had seen another side of Micah. She'd known he was a dedicated doctor, but she'd seen him interact with people on a personal level. Not only had he visited with Henry, but he had dropped by the rooms of others at the nursing home that he'd gotten to know over the years. He remembered them, and they remembered him. Before arriving at the home, he had stopped by a market and purchased fresh fruit for everyone, which they all seemed to enjoy.

Seeing them, especially the older men, made her realize that her father would one day get old and she would be his caretaker. He was in the best of health now, but he wasn't getting any younger. It also made her realize, more so than ever, just what a caring person Micah was.

She turned to Micah, who'd come to sit on the sofa across from her. "I'll prepare dinner tonight."

He raised an eyebrow. "You can cook?"

Kalina laughed. "Yes. I lived on my grandparents' farm in Alabama for a while, remember. They were big cooks and taught me my way around any kitchen. I just don't usually have a lot of time to do it when I'm working."

She glanced at her watch. "I think I'll cook a pot of spaghetti with a salad. Mind if I borrow the truck and go to that Walmart we passed on the way back to get some fresh ingredients?"

"No, I don't mind," he said, standing and pulling the truck keys from his pocket. His cousins had stocked his kitchen, but only with non-perishables. "Although you might want to check with Chloe or Pam. They probably have what you'll need since they like to cook."

"I'm sure they do, but I need to get a prescription filled anyway. I didn't think about it earlier while we were out."

"No problem. Do you want me to drive you?"

"No, I'll be fine." She stood. "And I won't be gone long."

"Glad to see that you're out of your foul mood, Micah," Derringer Westmoreland said with a grin as he fed one of the horses he kept in Micah's barn.

Micah shot him a dirty look, which any other man would have known meant he should zip it, but Derringer wasn't worried. He knew his cousin was not the hostile type. "I don't know what brought it on, but you need to chill. Save your frown for those contagious diseases."

Micah folded his arms across his chest. "And when did you become an expert on domestic matters, Derringer?"

Derringer chuckled. "On the day I married Lucia. I tell you, my life hasn't been the same since. Being married is good. You ought to try it."

Micah dropped his hands to his sides and shrugged. "I plan on it. I just have to get Kalina to trust me. She's got to get to know me better."

Derringer frowned, which didn't surprise Micah. Whereas Zane hadn't seen anything strange by that comment, Derringer would. "Doesn't she know you already?"

"Not the way I want her to. She thinks I betrayed her a couple of years ago, and I believe that once she gets to know me she'll see I'm not capable of doing anything like that."

Now it was Derringer who crossed his arms over his chest. "Wouldn't it be easier just to tell her that you didn't do it?"

"I tried that. It's her father's word against mine, and she chose to believe her father."

Derringer rubbed his chin in a thoughtful way. "You can always confront her old man and beat the truth out of him." He then glanced around. "And speaking of Kalina, where is she? I know the ladies decided not to do anything today since both Lucia and Chloe had to take the babies in for their regular pediatric visits."

"She's preparing dinner and needed to pick up a few items from the store." Micah checked his watch. "She's been gone longer than I figured she would be."

Concern touched Derringer's features. "You think she's gotten lost?"

"She shouldn't be lost since she was only going to that Walmart a few miles away. If she's not back in a few more minutes, I'll call her on her cell phone to make sure she's okay."

The two men had walked out of the barn when Micah's phone rang. He didn't recognize the number. "Yes?"

"Mr. Westmoreland, this is Nurse Nelson at Denver Memorial. There was a car accident involving Kalina Daniels, and she was brought into the emergency room. Your number was listed in her phone directory as one of those to call in case of an emergency. Since you're local we thought we would call you first."

Micah's heart stopped beating. "She was in an accident?"

"Yes."

"How is she?" he asked in a frantic tone.

"Not sure. The doctor is checking her out now."

Absently, Micah ended the call and looked at Derringer. "Kalina was in an accident, and she's been taken to Denver Memorial."

Derringer quickly tied the horse to the nearest post. "Come on. Let's go."

"Do you know an E.R. doctor's biggest nightmare?"

Kalina glanced over at the doctor who was checking out the bruise on her arm. "What?"

"Having to treat another doctor."

Kalina laughed. "Hey, I wasn't *that* bad, Dr. Parker."

"No." The older doctor nodded while grinning. "I understand you were worse. According to the paramedics, you wouldn't let them work on you until they'd checked out the person who was driving the other car. The one who ran the red light and caused the accident."

"Only because I knew I was fine. She's the one whose air bag deployed," Kalina said.

"Yes, but still, you deserved to be checked out as much as she did."

Kalina didn't say anything as she remembered the accident. She hadn't seen it coming. She had picked up all the things she needed from the store and was on her way back to Micah's Manor when out of nowhere, a car plowed into her from the side. She could only be thankful that she'd been driving Micah's heavy-duty truck and not a small car. Otherwise, her injuries would have been more severe.

"I don't like the look of this knot on your head. I should keep you overnight for observation."

Kalina shook her head. "Don't waste a bed. I'll be fine."

"Maybe. Maybe not. I don't have to tell you about head injuries, do I, Dr. Daniels?"

She rolled her eyes. "No, sir, you don't."

"Are you living alone?"

"No, I'm visiting someone in this area. I think your nurse has already called Micah."

The doctor looked at her. "Micah? Micah Westmoreland?"

Kalina smiled. "Yes. You know him?"

The doctor nodded. "Yes, I went to high school with his father. I know those Westmorelands well. It was tragic how they lost their parents, aunt and uncle in that plane crash."

"Yes, it was."

"The folks around here can't help admiring how they all stuck together in light of that devastation, and now all of them have made something of themselves, even Bane. God knows we'd almost given up on him, but now I understand that he's—"

Suddenly the privacy curtain was snatched aside, and Micah stood there with a terrified look on his face. "Kalina!"

And before she could draw her next breath, he had crossed the floor and pulled her into his arms.

Ten

Back at Micah's Manor, Kalina, who was sitting comfortably on the sofa, rolled her eyes. "If you ask me one more time if I'm okay, I'm going to scream. Read my lips, Micah. I'm fine."

Micah drew in a deep breath. He knew he was being anal, but he couldn't help it. When he'd received a call from that nurse about Kalina's accident, he'd lost it. It was a good thing Derringer had been there. There was probably no way he could have driven to the hospital without causing his own accident. He'd been that much of a basket case.

"Don't fall asleep, Kalina. If you do, I'm only going to wake you up," he warned.

She shook her head. "Micah, have you forgotten I'm a doctor, as well. I'm familiar with the dos and don'ts following a head injury. But, like I told Dr. Parker at the hospital, I'm fine."

"And I intend to make sure you stay that way." Micah crossed the room to her, leaned down and placed a kiss on her lips.

He straightened and glanced down at her. "I don't think you know how I felt when I received that call, Kal. It reminded me so much of the call I got that day from Dillon, telling me about Mom, Dad, Uncle Thomas and Aunt Susan. I was at the university, in between classes, and it seemed that everything went black."

She nodded slowly, hearing the pain in his voice. "I can imagine."

He shook his head. "No, honestly, you can't." He sat down beside her. "It was the kind of emotional pain and fear I'd hoped never to experience again. But I did today, when I got that call about you."

She stared at him for a few moments and then reached over and took his hand in hers. "Sorry. I didn't mean to do that to you."

He sighed deeply. "It wasn't your fault. Accidents happen. But if I didn't know before, I know now."

She lifted a brow. "You know what?"

"How much I care for you." He gently pulled her onto his lap. "I know you've been thinking that I've been acting moody and out of sorts for the past couple of days, but I wanted so much for you to believe I'm not the person you think I am."

She wrapped her arms around him, as well. "I know. And I also know that's why you didn't want to make love to me."

She twisted around in his arms to face him. "You

were wasting both our time by doing that, you know. I realized even before leaving India that you hadn't lied to me about our affair in Sydney."

He pulled back, surprised. "You had?"

"Yes. I had accepted what you said as the truth before I agreed to come here to Denver with you."

She smiled. "I figured that you *had* to be telling the truth, otherwise, you were taking a big risk in bringing me here to meet your family. But then I knew for a fact that you had been telling the truth once you got me here and wanted to put a hold on our lovemaking. You were willing to do without something I knew you really wanted just to prove yourself to me. You really didn't have to."

He covered her hand with his. "I felt that I did have to do it. Someone once told me that sacrifices today will result in dividends tomorrow, and I wanted you for my dividend. I love you, Kalina."

"And I love you, too. I realized that before coming here, as well. That night you took me dancing and I felt something in the way you held me, in the way you were talking to me. That night, I knew the truth in what you had been trying to tell me. And I knew the truth about what my feelings were for you."

She quieted for a moment and then said, "Although there's not an excuse for my father's actions, I believe I know why he did what he did. He's always been controlling, but I never thought he would go that far. I was wrong. And I was wrong for not believing you in the first place."

He shook his head. "No, like I said, you didn't know me. We had an affair that was purely sexual. The only commitment we'd made was to share a bed. It didn't take me long to figure out that I wanted more from you. That night you ended things was the night I had planned on telling you how I felt. Afterward, I was angry that you didn't believe in me, that you actually thought I didn't care, that I would go along with your father about something like that."

He paused. "When I came home, I told Dillon everything and he suggested that I straighten things out. But my pride wouldn't let me. I wasted two years being angry, but the night I saw you again I knew that no matter what, I would make you mine."

"No worries then," Kalina said, reaching up and cupping his chin. "I am yours."

He inhaled sharply when her fingers slid beneath his T-shirt to touch his naked skin over his heart. It seemed the moment she touched him that heat consumed him and spread to every part of his body. Although he tried playing it down, his desire for her was magnified to a level he hadn't thought possible.

All he could think about was that he'd almost lost her and the fear that had lodged in his throat had made it difficult to breathe. And now she was here, back at his manor, where she belonged. He knew then that he would always protect her. Not control her like her old man tended to do, but to protect her.

"Make love to me, Micah."

Her whispered request swept across his lips. "I need you inside me."

Micah studied her thoughtfully. He saw the heat in her eyes and felt the feverishness of her skin. Other than that one time on the sofa, he hadn't touched her since coming to Denver, wanting her to get to know the real him. Well, at that moment, the real him wanted her with a passion that he felt even in the tips of his fingers. She knew him, and she loved him, just as he loved her.

"What about your head?" he whispered, standing, sweeping her into his arms and moving toward the stairs.

She wrapped her arms around him and chuckled against his neck. "My head is fine, but there is another ache that's bothering me. To be quite honest with you, it was bothering me a long time before the accident. It's the way my body is aching to be touched by you. Loved by you. Needed by you."

Just how he made it up the stairs to his bedroom, he wasn't sure. All he knew was that he had placed her in the middle of his bed, stripped off her clothes and taken off his own clothes in no time at all. He stood at the foot of the bed, gazing at her. He let his eyes roam all over her and knew there was nothing subtle about how he was doing it.

This was the first time she had been in his bed, but he had fantasized about her being here plenty of times. Even during the last five days, when he'd known she was sleeping in the bedroom above his, he had wanted her here, with him. More than once, he had been tempted to get up during the night and go to her, to forget about the promise of not touching her until she had gotten to know him. It had been hard wanting her and vowing not to touch her.

And she hadn't made it easy. At times she had deliberately tried tempting him again. She would go shopping with his cousins and then parade around in some of the sexiest outfits a store could sell. But he had resisted temptation.

But not now. He didn't plan on resisting anything,

especially not the naked woman stretched out in the middle of his huge bed looking as if she belonged there. He intended to keep her there.

"I love you," he said in a low, gravelly voice filled with so much emotion he had to fight from getting choked. "I knew I did, but I didn't know just how much until I got that phone call, Kalina. You are my heart. My soul. My very reason for existing."

He slowly moved toward the bed. "I never knew how much I cherished this part of our relationship until it was gone. I can't go back and see it as 'just sex' anymore. Not when I can distinctly hear, in the back of my mind, all your moans of pleasure, the way you groan to let me know how much you want me. Not when I remember that little smile that lets me know just how much you are satisfied. No, we never had sex. We've always made love."

Kalina breathed in Micah's scent as he moved closer to her. Not wanting to wait any longer, she rose up in the bed and met him. When he placed his knee on the bed, they tumbled back into the bedcovers together. At that moment, everything ceased to exist except them.

As if she needed to make sure this moment was real, she reached out and touched his face, using her fingertips to caress the strong lines of his features. But she didn't stop there, she trailed her fingers down to his chest, feeling the hard muscles of his stomach. Her hands moved even lower, to the hardest part of him, cupping him. She thought, for someone to be so hard, there were certain parts of him that were smooth as a baby's behind.

"What are you doing to me?" he asked in a tortured groan when she continued to stroke him.

She met his gaze. "Staking my claim."

He chuckled softly. "Baby, trust me. You staked your claim two years ago. I haven't been able to make love to another woman since."

Micah knew the moment she realized the truth of what he'd said. The smile that touched her features warmed him all over, made him appreciate that he was a man, the man who had *this* woman.

Not being able to wait any longer, he leaned over and brushed a kiss against her lips. Then he moved his mouth lower to capture a nipple in his mouth and suck on it.

She arched against him, and he appreciated her doing so. He increased the suction of his mouth, relishing the taste of her while thinking of all the hours he'd lain in this bed awake and aroused, knowing she'd been only one floor away.

"Micah."

The tone of her voice alerted him that she needed him inside that part of her that was aching. Releasing her nipple, he eased her down in the bed. Before he moved in place between her legs, he had to taste her. He shifted his body to bury his head between her legs.

Kalina screamed the moment Micah's tongue swept inside her. The tip of it was hot and determined. And the way it swirled inside her had her senses swirling in unison. She was convinced that no other man could do things with their tongue the way he could. He was devouring her senseless, and she couldn't do anything but lie there and moan.

And then she felt it, an early sign that a quake was about to happen. The way her toes began tingling while her head crested with sensations that moved through every part of her.

She sucked in a deep breath, and it was then that she saw he had sensed what was about to happen and had moved in place over her. The hardness of him slid through her wetness, filling her and going beyond.

She was well aware of the moment when their bodies locked. He gazed down at her, and their eyes connected. He was about to give her the ride of her life, and she needed it. She wanted it.

He began moving, thrusting in and out of her while holding her gaze. She felt it. She felt him. There was nothing like the feeling of being made love to by the one man who had your heart. Your soul.

He kept moving, thrusting, pounding into her as if making up for lost time, for misunderstandings and disagreements. She wouldn't delude herself into thinking those things wouldn't happen again, but now they would have love to cushion the blows.

At that moment, he deliberately curved his body to hit her at an angle that made her G-spot weep. It triggered her scream, and she exploded at the same time as he did. They clung to each other, limbs entwined, bodies united. She sucked up air along with his scent. And moments later, when the last remnants of the blast flittered away from her, she collapsed against Micah, moaning his name and knowing she had finally christened his bed.

Their bed.

The next two weeks flowed smoothly, although they were busy ones for the Westmoreland family. Gemma and Callum were returning to christen their firstborn. Ramsey and Chloe had consented to be godparents.

All the out-of-towners were scheduled to arrive by Thursday. Most had made plans to stay at nearby hotels, but others were staying with family members. Jason and his wife, Bella, had turned what had been the home she'd inherited from her grandfather into a private inn just for family when they came to visit.

Pam had solicited Kalina's help in planning activities for everyone, and Kalina appreciated being included. Her days were kept busy, but her nights remained exclusively for Micah. They rode horses around the property every evening, cooked dinner together, took their shower, once in a while watched a movie. But every night they shared a bed. She thought there was nothing like waking up each morning in his arms.

Like this morning.

She glanced over at him and frowned. "Just look what you did to me. What if I wanted to wear a low-cut dress?"

Micah glanced over at the passion mark he'd left on Kalina. Right there on her breast. There was not even a hint of remorse in his voice when he said, "Then I guess you'd be changing outfits."

"Oh, you!" she said, snatching the pillow and throwing it at him. "You probably did it deliberately. You like branding me."

He couldn't deny her charge because it was true. But what he liked most of all was tasting her. Unfortunately, he had a tendency to leave a mark whenever he did. Hell, he couldn't help that she tasted so damn good.

He reached out and grabbed her before she could

toss another pillow his way. "Come here, sweetheart. Let me kiss it away."

"All you're going to do is make another mark. Stay away from me."

He rolled his eyes. "Yeah. Right."

When she tried scooting away, he grabbed her foot to bring her back. He then lowered his mouth to lick her calf. When she moaned, he said, "See, you know you like it."

"Yes, but we don't have the time. Everyone starts arriving today."

"Let them. They can wait."

When he released his hold on her to grab her around the waist, she used that opportunity to scoot away from him and quickly made a move to get out of bed. But she wasn't quick enough. He grabbed her arm and pulled her back. "Did you think you would get away, Dr. Daniels?"

She couldn't help laughing, and she threw herself into his arms. "It's not like I'm ready to get out of bed anyway," she said, before pressing her lips to his. He kissed her the way she liked, in a way that sent sensations escalating all through her.

When he released her lips she felt a tug on her left hand and looked down. She sucked in a deep breath at the beautiful diamond ring Micah had just slid on her finger. She threw her hand to her chest to stop the rapid beating of her heart. "Oh, my God!

Micah chuckled as he brought her ringed hand to his lips and kissed it. "Will you, Kalina Marie Daniels, marry me? Will you live here with me at Micah's Manor? Have my babies? Make me the happiest man on earth?"

Tears streamed down her face, and she tried swiping them away, but more kept coming. "Oh, Micah, yes! Yes! I'll marry you, live here and have your babies."

Micah laughed and pulled her into his arms, sealing her promise with another kiss.

It was much later when they left Micah's Manor to head over to Dillon's place. Dillon had called to say the Atlanta Westmorelands had begun arriving already. Micah had put his brother on the speakerphone and Kalina could hear the excitement in Dillon's voice. It didn't take long, when around the Westmorelands, to know that family meant everything to them. They enjoyed the times they were able to get together.

Micah had explained that all the Westmorelands were making up for the years they hadn't shared when they hadn't known about each other. Their dedication to family was the reason it was important to make sure there weren't any other Westmorelands out there they didn't know about.

Kalina walked into Dillon and Pam's house with Micah by her side and a ring on her finger. Several family members noticed her diamond and congratulated them and asked when the big day would be. She and Micah both wanted a June wedding, which was less than a couple of months away.

Once they walked into the living room, Kalina suddenly came to a stop. Several people were standing around talking. Micah's arm tightened around her shoulders and he glanced down at her. "What's wrong, baby?"

Instead of answering, she stared across the room and

he followed her gaze. Immediately, he knew what was bothering her.

"That woman is here," was all Kalina would say.

Micah couldn't help fighting back a smile as he gazed over at Olivia. "Yes, she's here, and I think it's time for you to meet her."

Kalina began backing up slowly. "I'd rather not do that."

"And if you don't, my cousin Senator Reggie Westmoreland will wonder why you're deliberately being rude to his wife."

Kalina jerked her head up and looked at Micah. "His wife?"

Micah couldn't hold back his smile any longer. "Yes, his wife. That's Olivia Jeffries Westmoreland."

"But you had me thinking that—"

Micah reached out and quickly kissed the words from Kalina's lips. "Don't place the blame on me, sweetheart. You assumed Olivia and I had something going on. I never told you that. In fact, I recall telling you that there was nothing going on with us. Olivia and Reggie had invited me to lunch while I was in D.C., but it was Olivia who came to pick me up that day. I couldn't help that you got jealous."

She glared. "I didn't get jealous."

"Didn't you?"

He stared at her, and she stared back. Then a slow smile spread across her face, and she shrugged her shoulders. "Okay, maybe I did. But just a little."

He raised a dubious eyebrow. "Um, just a little."

"Don't press it, Micah."

He laughed and tightened his hand on hers. "Okay, I won't. Come on and meet Reggie, Olivia and their twin sons, as well as the rest of my cousins. And I think we should announce our good news."

The christening for Callum Austell II was a beautiful ceremony, and Kalina got to meet Micah's cousin Gemma. She couldn't wait to tell her just how gifted she was as an interior designer, which prompted Gemma to share how her husband had whisked her off to Australia in the first place.

It was obvious to anyone around them that Gemma and her husband were in love and that they shared a happy marriage. But then, Kalina thought, the same thing could be said for all of Micah's cousins' marriages. All the men favored each other, and the women they'd selected as their mates complemented them.

After the church service, dinner was served at the big house with all the women pitching in and cooking. Kalina felt good knowing the games she had organized for everyone, especially the kids, had been a big hit.

It was late when she and Micah had finally made it back to Micah's Manor. After a full day of being around the Westmorelands, she should have been exhausted, ready to fall on her face, but she felt wired and had Micah telling her the story about Raphel all over again. She was even more fascinated with it the second time.

"That's how Dillon and Pam met," Micah said as they headed up the stairs. An hour or so later, he and Kalina had showered together and were settling down to watch a movie in bed, when the phone rang.

He glanced over at the clock. "I wonder who's calling this late," he said, reaching for the phone. "Probably Megan wanting to know if we still have any of that ice cream she bought."

He picked up the phone. "Hello."

"Are you watching television, Micah?"

He heard the urgency in Dillon's voice. "I just turned it on to watch a DVD, why?"

"I think you ought to switch to CNN. There's something going on in Oregon."

Micah raised a brow. "Oregon?"

"Yes. It's like people are falling dead in the streets for no reason."

Micah was out of the bed in a flash. He looked at Kalina, who had the remote in her hand. "Switch to CNN."

She did so, and Anderson Cooper's face flared to life on the screen as he said, "No one is sure what is happening here, but it's like a scene out of *Contagion*. So far, more than ten people have died. The Centers for Disease Control has…"

At that moment Micah's phone on his dresser, the one with a direct line to Washington, rang. He moved quickly to pick it up. "Yes?"

He looked over at Kalina and nodded. Her gaze held his, knowing whenever that particular phone rang it was urgent. "All right, we're on our way."

He clicked off. "They're calling the entire team in. We're needed in Oregon."

Eleven

Micah looked around the huge room. His team was reunited. Kalina, Theo and Beau. They had all read the report and knew what they were up against. The Centers for Disease Control had called in an international team and the three of them were just a part of it. But in his mind they were a major part. All the evidence collected pointed to a possible terrorist attack. If they didn't get a grip on what was happening and stop it, the effect could make 9/11 look small in comparison.

It didn't take long to see, from the tissue taken from some of the victims, that they were dealing with the same kind of virus that he, Kalina and Theo had investigated in India just weeks ago. How did it get to the States? And, more important, who was responsible for spreading it?

He felt his phone vibrating in his pocket and didn't

have to pull it out to see who was calling. It was the same person who'd been blowing up his phone for the past two days. General Daniels. He was demanding that Kalina be sent home, out of harm's way. Like two years ago, a part of Micah understood the man's concern for his daughter's safety. He, of all people, didn't want a single hair on Kalina's head hurt in any way. But as much as he loved Kalina and wanted to keep her safe, he also respected her profession and her choices in life. That's how he and the old man differed.

But still…

"That's all for now. I'll give everyone an update when I get one from Washington. Stay safe." Micah then glanced over at Kalina. "Dr. Daniels, can you remain a few moments, please? I'd like to talk to you."

He moved behind his desk as the others filed out. Beau, being the last one, closed the door behind him. But not before giving Micah the eye, communicating to him, for his own benefit and safety, to move the vase off the desk. Micah smiled. Beau knew of Kalina's need to throw things when she was angry. He had tried telling his best friend that the vase throwing had been limited to that one episode. It hadn't happened again.

"Yes, Micah? What is it?"

He pulled his still-vibrating phone out of his pocket and placed it in the middle of his desk. "Your father."

He then reached into his desk and pulled out a sealed, official-looking envelope and handed it to her. "Your father, as well."

She opened the envelope and began reading the documents. Moments later, she lifted her head and met his gaze. "Orders for me to be reassigned to another project?"

"Yes."

She held his gaze for a long time as she placed the documents back in the envelope. He saw the defeated shift of her shoulders. "So when do I leave?"

He leaned back in his chair. "I, of all people, don't want anything to happen to you, Kalina," he said in a low voice. "I love you more than life itself, and I know how dangerous it is for you to be here. The death toll has gone up to fifteen. Already a domestic terrorist group is claiming victory and vows more people will lose their lives here before it's over, before we can find a way to stop it. I don't want you in that number."

There was an intensity, a desperation, in his tone that even he heard. It was also one that he felt. He drew in a deep breath and continued, "You are the other half that makes me whole. The sunshine I wake up to each morning, and the rock I hold near me when I go to bed at night. I don't want to lose you. If anything happens to you, I die, as well."

He could see she was fighting the tears in her eyes, as if she already knew the verdict. She was getting used to it. She lifted her chin defiantly. "So, you're sending me away?"

He held his gaze as he shook his head. "No, I'm keeping you safe. Your father doesn't call the shots anymore in your personal or professional life. I'm denying his orders on the grounds that you're needed here. You worked on this virus just weeks ago. You're familiar with it. That alone should override his request at the CDC."

She released an appreciative sigh. "Thank you."

"Don't thank me. The next days are going to be rough. Whoever did this is out there and waiting around for their attack to be successful. There have been few survivors and those who have survived are quarantined and in critical condition."

She sat down on the edge of his desk. "We're working against time, Micah. People want to leave Portland, but everyone is being forced to stay because the virus is contagious."

Already the level of fear among citizens had been raised. People were naturally afraid of the unknown… and this was definitely an unknown. Each victim had presented the same symptoms they'd found in India.

"I wish the CDC hadn't just put that blood sample I sent to them on the shelf," she added. "It was the one thing I was able to get from the surviving—"

Micah sat up in his seat. "Hey, that might be it. We need someone to analyze the contents of those vials, immediately. I don't give a damn about how behind they are. This is urgent." He picked up the phone that was a direct line to Washington and the Department of Health and Human Services.

Four more people died over a two-day period, but Micah put the fire under the CDC to study the contents of those vials that Kalina had sent to them weeks ago. He had assembled his team in the lab to apprise them of what was going on.

"And you think we might be able to come up with a serum that can stop the virus?" Beau asked.

"We hope so," Micah said, rubbing a hand down his face. "It might be a shot in the dark, but it's the only one we have."

At that moment, the phone—his direct line to the

CDC—rang, and he quickly picked it up. "Dr. West-moreland."

He nodded a few times and then he felt a relieved expression touch his features. "Great! You get it here, and we'll dispense it."

He looked over at his team. "Based on what they analyzed in those vials, they think they've come up with an antidote. They're flying it here via military aircraft. We are to work with the local teams and make sure every man, woman and child is inoculated imme-diately." He stood. "Let's go!"

Five days later, a military aircraft carrying Micah and his team arrived at Andrews Air Force Base. The antidote had worked, and millions of lives were saved. Homeland Security had arrested those involved.

Micah and every member of his team had worked nonstop to save lives and thanks to their hard work, and the work of all the others, there hadn't been anymore deaths.

He drew in a deep breath as he glanced over at Kalina. He knew how exhausted she was, though she didn't show it. All of them had kept long hours, and he was looking forward to a hotel room with a big bed… and his woman. They would rest up, and then they would ease into much-needed lovemaking.

They had barely departed the plane when an offi-cial government vehicle pulled up. They paused, and Micah really wasn't surprised when Kalina's father got out of the car. General Daniels frowned at them. All military personnel there saluted and stood at attention as he moved toward them.

As much as Micah wanted to hate the man, he

couldn't. After all, he was Kalina's father and without
the man his daughter would not have been born. So
Micah figured that he owed the older man something.
That was all he could find to like about him. At the
moment, he couldn't think of a single other thing.

General Daniels came to a stop in front of them.
"Dr. Westmoreland. I need to congratulate you and your
team for a job well done."

"Thank you, sir." Micah decided to give the man the
respect he had earned. Considering the lie the man had
told, whether he really deserved it was another matter.

The general's gaze shifted to Kalina, and Micah
knew where she had gotten her stubbornness. She lifted
her chin and glared at her father, general or not. Micah
noticed something else, as well. It was there in the
older man's eyes as he looked at Kalina. He loved his
daughter and was scared to death of losing her. Kalina
had told him how her mother had died when she was ten
and how hard her father had taken her mother's death.

"Kalina Marie."

"General."

"You look well."

"Thank you."

The general spoke to all the others and then offi-
cially dismissed them to leave. He then said to Kalina
when the three of them were alone. "I'm here to take
you and Dr. Westmoreland to your hotel."

Kalina's glare deepened. "I'll walk first. Sir."

Micah saw the pain from Kalina's words settle in
the old man's eyes. He decided to extend something to
General Daniels that the old man would never extend
to him: empathy.

He then turned to Kalina and said in a joking tone,

"No, you aren't walking to the hotel because that means I'll have to walk with you. We're a team, remember? And if I take another step, I'm going to drop. I think we should take your father up on his offer. Besides, there're a couple things we need to talk to him about, don't you think? Like our wedding plans."

The general blinked. "The two of you are back together? And getting married?"

Kalina turned on her father. "Yes, with no thanks to you."

The man did have the decency to look chagrined. Micah had a feeling the man truly felt regret for his actions two years ago. "And there's something else I think you should tell your father, Kalina."

She glanced up at Micah. "What?"

Micah smiled. "That he's going to be a grandfather."

Both Kalina and her father gasped in shock, but for different reasons. Kalina turned to Micah. "You knew?"

He nodded as his smile widened. "Yes, I'm a doctor, remember."

"And you still let me stay on the team? You didn't send me away, knowing my condition?"

He reached out and gently caressed her cheek. "You were under my love and protection, but not my control."

He then looked over at her father when he added, "There is a difference, General, and one day I'll be happy to sit down and explain it to you."

The old man nodded appreciatively and held Micah's gaze as a deep understanding and acceptance passed between them.

"But right now, I'd like to be taken to the nearest

hotel. I plan on sleeping for the next five days," Micah said, moving toward the government car.

"With me right beside you," Kalina added as she walked with him. She figured she'd gotten pregnant during the time the doctor had placed her on antibiotics after the auto accident. Even as a medical professional, it hadn't crossed her mind that the prescribed medicine would have a negative effect on her birth control pills. There had been too much going on for her emotionally at the time. Since she'd found out, she had been waiting for the perfect time to tell Micah that he would be a father. And to think, he'd suspected all the time.

Micah took Kalina's hand in his, immediately feeling the heat that always seemed to generate between them. This was his woman, soon to be his wife and the mother of his child. Life couldn't be better.

Epilogue

Two months later, on a hot June day, Micah and Kalina stood before a minister on the grounds of Micah's Manor and listened when a minister proclaimed, "I now pronounce you man and wife."

All the Westmorelands had returned to help celebrate on their beautiful day.

"You may now kiss your bride."

Micah pulled Kalina into his arms and gave her a kiss she had come to know, love and expect. He released her from the kiss only when a couple of his brothers and cousins began clearing their throats.

With the help of Pam, Lucia, Bella, Megan, Bailey and Chloe, Kalina had found the perfect wedding dress. She'd also formed relationships with the women she now considered sisters. Kalina and Micah's honeymoon to Paris was a nice wedding gift—compliments of her father.

And Bella had taken time to give birth to beautiful identical twin daughters. And Ramsey and Chloe now had a son who was the spitting image of his father. Already, the fathers, uncles and cousins were spoiling them rotten. Kalina had to admit she was in that number, and couldn't wait to hold her own baby in her arms.

A short while later, at the reception, Kalina glanced over at her husband. He was such a handsome man, dashing as ever in his tux. More than one person had said that they made a beautiful couple.

She had been pulled to the side and was talking to the ladies when suddenly the group got quiet. Everyone turned when an extremely handsome man got out of a car. The first thing Kalina thought, with his dashing good looks, was that perhaps he was some Hollywood celebrity who was a friend of one of Micah's cousins, especially since it seemed all the male Westmorelands knew who he was.

When Micah approached and touched her hand she glanced up at him and smiled. She hadn't been aware he had returned to her side. "Who's that?" she asked curiously.

He followed her gaze and chuckled. "That's Rico Claiborne. Savannah and Jessica's brother."

Kalina nodded. Savannah and Jessica were sisters who'd married the Westmoreland cousins Durango and Chase. "He's handsome," she couldn't help saying. Then she quickly looked up at her husband and added sheepishly, "But not as handsome as you, of course."

Micah laughed. "Of course. Here, I brought this for you," he said, placing a cold glass of ice water in her hand. "And although Megan is hiring Rico, they are meeting for the first time today," he added. "But from the expression on Megan's face, maybe she needs this cold drink of water instead of you."

Kalina understood exactly what Micah meant when she, like everyone else, watched as the man turned to stare over at Megan, who'd been pointed out to him by some of the Westmoreland cousins. If the look on Megan's face, and the look on the man's face when he saw Megan, was anything to go by, then everyone was feeling the heat.

Kalina took a sip of her seltzer water thinking that Micah was right. Megan should be the one drinking the cooling beverage instead of her.

"Are you ready for our honeymoon, sweetheart?"

Micah's question reclaimed her attention and she smiled up at him, Megan and the hottie private investigator forgotten already. "Yes, I'm ready."

And she was. She was more than ready to start sharing her life with the man she loved.

* * * * *

PASSION

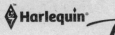

COMING NEXT MONTH
AVAILABLE MAY 8, 2012

#2155 UNDONE BY HER TENDER TOUCH
Pregnancy & Passion
Maya Banks
When one night with magnate Cam Hollingsworth results in pregnancy, no-strings-attached turns into a tangled web for caterer Pippa Laingley.

#2156 ONE DANCE WITH THE SHEIKH
Dynasties: The Kincaids
Tessa Radley

#2157 THE TIES THAT BIND
Billionaires and Babies
Emilie Rose

#2158 AN INTIMATE BARGAIN
Colorado Cattle Barons
Barbara Dunlop

#2159 RELENTLESS PURSUIT
Lone Star Legacy
Sara Orwig

#2160 READY FOR HER CLOSE-UP
Matchmakers, Inc.
Katherine Garbera

HDCNM0412

REQUEST YOUR FREE BOOKS!
2 FREE NOVELS PLUS 2 FREE GIFTS!

Harlequin

Desire

ALWAYS POWERFUL, PASSIONATE AND PROVOCATIVE

YES! Please send me 2 FREE Harlequin Desire® novels and my 2 FREE gifts (gifts are worth about $10). After receiving them, if I don't wish to receive any more books, I can return the shipping statement marked "cancel." If I don't cancel, I will receive 6 brand-new novels every month and be billed just $4.30 per book in the U.S. or $4.99 per book in Canada. That's a saving of at least 14% off the cover price! It's quite a bargain! Shipping and handling is just 50¢ per book in the U.S. and 75¢ per book in Canada.* I understand that accepting the 2 free books and gifts places me under no obligation to buy anything. I can always return a shipment and cancel at any time. Even if I never buy another book, the two free books and gifts are mine to keep forever.

225/326 HDN FEF3

Name	(PLEASE PRINT)
Address	Apt. #
City	State/Prov. Zip/Postal Code

Signature (if under 18, a parent or guardian must sign)

Mail to the **Reader Service:**
IN U.S.A.: P.O. Box 1867, Buffalo, NY 14240-1867
IN CANADA: P.O. Box 609, Fort Erie, Ontario L2A 5X3

Not valid for current subscribers to Harlequin Desire books.

Want to try two free books from another line?
Call 1-800-873-8635 or visit www.ReaderService.com.

* Terms and prices subject to change without notice. Prices do not include applicable taxes. Sales tax applicable in N.Y. Canadian residents will be charged applicable taxes. Offer not valid in Quebec. This offer is limited to one order per household. All orders subject to credit approval. Credit or debit balances in a customer's account(s) may be offset by any other outstanding balance owed by or to the customer. Please allow 4 to 6 weeks for delivery. Offer available while quantities last.

Your Privacy—The Reader Service is committed to protecting your privacy. Our Privacy Policy is available online at www.ReaderService.com or upon request from the Reader Service.

We make a portion of our mailing list available to reputable third parties that offer products we believe may interest you. If you prefer that we not exchange your name with third parties, or if you wish to clarify or modify your communication preferences, please visit us at www.ReaderService.com/consumerschoice or write to us at Reader Service Preference Service, P.O. Box 9062, Buffalo, NY 14269. Include your complete name and address.

He never saw her coming....

A red-hot tale of passion and danger from
New York Times bestselling author

LORI FOSTER

Spencer Lark already knows
too many secrets about Arizona
Storm, including the nightmare
she survived and her resulting
trust issues. But in order to
expose a smuggling ring—and
continue avenging his own
tragic past—the bounty hunter
reluctantly agrees to make
Arizona a decoy. Yet nothing has
equipped him for her hypnotic
blend of fragility and bravery, or
for the protective instincts she
stirs in him....

"Lori Foster delivers the goods."
—*Publishers Weekly*

A PERFECT STORM

Available now.

"**W**ould you like some help?"

Pippa whirled around, still holding the bottle of champagne, and darn near tossed the contents onto the floor.

"Help?"

Cam nodded slowly. "Assistance? You look as though you could use it. How on earth did you think you'd manage to cater this event on your own?"

Pippa was horrified by his offer and then, as she processed the rest of his statement, she was irritated as hell.

"I'd hate for you to sully those pretty hands," she snapped. "And for your information, I've got this under control. The help didn't show. Not my fault. The food is impeccable, if I do say so myself. I just need to deliver it to the guests."

"I believe I just offered my assistance and you insulted me," Cam said dryly.

Her eyebrows drew together. Oh, why did the man have to be so damn delicious-looking? And why could she never perform the simplest functions around him?

"You're Ashley's guest," Pippa said firmly. "Not to mention you're used to being served, not serving others."

"How do you know what I'm used to?" he asked mildly.

She had absolutely nothing to say to that and watched in bewilderment as he hefted the tray up and walked out of the kitchen.

She sagged against the sink, her pulse racing hard enough

to make her dizzy.

Cameron Hollingsworth was gorgeous, unpolished in a rough and totally sexy way, arrogant and so wrong for her. But there was something about the man that just did it for her.

She sighed. He was a luscious specimen of a male and he couldn't be any less interested in her.

Even so, she was itching to shake his world up a little.

Realizing she was spending far too much time mooning over Cameron, she grabbed another tray, took a deep breath to compose herself and then headed toward the living room.

And Cameron Hollingsworth.

Will Pippa shake up Cameron's world?
Find out in Maya Banks's passionate new novel

UNDONE BY HER TENDER TOUCH

Available May 2012 from Harlequin® Desire!

Coming soon, a brand-new Madaris Family novel!

NEW YORK TIMES BESTSELLING AUTHOR

BRENDA JACKSON

COURTING JUSTICE

A Madaris Family Novel

Sometimes the only crime is
giving in to temptation...

Pick up your copy on May 29, 2012, wherever books are sold!

KIMANI PRESS™
www.kimanipress.com

KPBJ53473